A Matter of Truth

BRIGETTE MANIE

DEDICATION

To God for inspiration and my family for their support.

Other Titles in the Seneca Mountain Romance Series

CHAPTER I

She expected a miracle from a God she didn't serve. How presumptuous was that? Elizabeth Monroe thought about asking Dr. Fields to repeat the diagnosis. Maybe the answer would be different the second time around. If only she could be so fortunate.

"I see that you need some time to process the news," the doctor said kindly.

Time plus eternity wouldn't be enough. Elizabeth gave her a tight smile. She wondered if she could trade bodies and her dilemma with the African American doctor she'd found online. With her problem, she hadn't wanted to see her regular physician, who happened to go to her church. Her situation needed to be hidden from the saints, even if they were professionals and bound by ethics to keep her confidence.

"You know that there are other options, right?" the woman continued when Elizabeth didn't speak.

She shuddered at the thought of what Dr. Fields meant. She could NOT do that! Guilty of coveting her neighbor's husband and of fornication, her sins were mounting. Very likely she was also guilty of having another God besides Jehovah, with the way she'd idolized Terence over their two-year involvement that ended three weeks ago. She was not prepared to break one more commandment.

Elizabeth lifted her purse from the seat beside her and stood. "Thank you, doctor," she said, reaching across the gleaming oak desk to shake the woman's hand.

"Remember to fill the prescription I gave you." Dr. Fields smiled and shook her hand.

As if she could forget. She may not want this problem, but she had to take care of it. Elizabeth left the doctor's office and stepped out into Monday morning July heat. Humidity, thicker than mud, sat in the air, the weight of it pulling moisture from every living thing. She hurried to her Acura, eager for the air-conditioned relief it would provide. Elizabeth sat for a while, staring into the busy parking lot of the large medical complex in downtown Mountain Spring. What was she going to do? A red SUV rolled out of a parking space. A white Mercedes Benz grabbed the vacancy, the paint of the car a stark contrast to the vehicle that left. Stark. *Now there's a word that applies to me.* Stark, raving mad. If she wasn't careful, that's how she'd end up.

She had to plan, had to find a way to take care of this—a fast fix. Sleeping with a married man had been a secret sin. This, what she was going through now, wouldn't be a secret, at least not for much longer. Elizabeth didn't think she could endure the shame, the whispers, and the disappointment when her private carelessness showed its very public consequence. She knew of only one way to prevent that—well, only one usable solution, which would allow her to face herself in the mirror every morning.

***

Later that evening around sunset, Elizabeth turned the corner of her apartment building and walked smack into someone who set her solution afire and sent it up in perfect smoke. Terence!

"Hi, Liz." He smiled and her heart staggered, synchronizing with the shaking in her knees.

"W-what are you doing here?" she croaked. Her eyes consumed him—a six-foot, five-inch wall of broad shoulders, muscular arms, boulder-solid abs, and powerful legs. One look and her three-week buried desire resurrected.

"I wanted to talk to you."

"I-I thought we were done doing that." The sunset's orange rays kissed his amber skin and turned it to burnished bronze, strengthening his appeal and stirring her attraction to him.

"So did I, but I miss you, Liz."

His low, husky pitch caressed her highly sensitive nerves and stoked a banked need for him, which she had suppressed by force.

"Terence, we ended this—you did and I accepted. Let's not return to what we both know is wrong." Elizabeth felt good that she delivered the line in a steady voice. She tried to step around him, but he caught her arm.

"Can we just talk?"

"Let me go before someone notices, especially someone we know," she warned.

"Let's go to your apartment," he proposed, starting to urge her in that direction.

"No," she resisted, standing her ground, "that's a bad idea."

"Staying out here where somebody who knows us can see *is* a bad idea."

"Then you shouldn't have come."

"Liz, all I want to do is talk to you," he appealed. "Can we please go inside?"

Reason said she should walk away and leave him right where he stood. But as she watched a coaxing smile tease around his lips, along with the puppy-pleading look in his eyes, her will to speak a negative washed away.

Inside her apartment, Elizabeth walked to the center of the living room and stood by one of her two ivory armchairs.

Terence stopped three feet away and stunned her with his first words, "Liz, I want you back."

He went on when she kept staring at him, "I thought I could let you go, thought I could do without being with you, but I can't."

"Not even for your kids?" It was the main line he'd fed her for their break up. He couldn't risk continuing an affair with her, for if his wife found out, he'd end up in divorce and lose his kids. She went over every word he'd just spoken and realized the word 'I' preceded each statement. This was all about him and what he wanted. What? Did he realize that despite his good intentions of being a family man, he wanted the sex he couldn't get from Sonja, so to hell with the kids? He'd spoken to her about his wife's overweight and undesirable condition, had blamed it as the cause for him 'stepping out.' At the time he told her that, she'd been

3

involved with him already and in love, too, so she hadn't dwelt much on how shallow and selfish he was. Now that she was pregnant for him and had to carry the burden alone, Elizabeth felt irritated at his self-centeredness.

"My kids won't find out, and Sonja won't know. We'll be more careful than before," he promised like that would guarantee they were never discovered. "We'll go to hotels out of Mountain Spring, instead of meeting at your place late at night." He smiled and stepped closer, taking her silence for agreement.

"*We?*" Elizabeth stressed with scorn, her temper igniting at his presumption and egotism. "You ended *us* three weeks ago, remember?"

"Liz, that was a mistake," he said, moving close enough now for her to see the tiny crow's feet at the corner of his left eye.

"What's a mistake is your coming over here tonight," she said, raising her voice.

"Don't get mad," he soothed, reaching out to caress her cheek.

She jerked away from his touch. He let his hand fall to his side, but his confident smile remained as he added, "I came to let you know that I want us to get back together."

Elizabeth studied Terence and gave him an ultimatum that she didn't believe in. "Okay, if you want us to be together, divorce Sonja and marry me."

That killed his cocky grin. "Liz, you know I can't do that. I have my kids to think about. A divorce would harm them."

"And them finding out about your cheating with me won't?"

"They'll never find out. We just have to be super discreet."

"This sounds like everybody's protected and satisfied, except me," Elizabeth declared with disgust. "You get sex, and your wife and kids never find out because we're *discreet*," she said, her lips curling scornfully around the final word.

"You make it sound despicable," he chided.

"It is rotten, low-down, and filthy," Elizabeth bit out. "And I want no part of it."

"Liz, you know you don't mean that. Both of us enjoyed what we had together; neither of us wanted it to end."

Elizabeth spoke words that she should have said a long time ago. "What we enjoyed was forbidden sexual intercourse. You are a married man. I'm a single woman. We're both supposed to be Christians. You and I know that God isn't pleased with this carnality."

Losing his coercive tactics, he said sarcastically, "It took you two years and countless nights of you screaming my name when I brought you to a climax for you to realize that?"

Her heart thumped at his reference to what they'd done together, and Elizabeth experienced shame as her flesh jumped at the memory his words revived. In her head, she understood that what they'd done together was wrong, but her body broadcasted another message. She had a clear understanding of what Paul meant when he said in Romans 7:19 that the good he would do eluded him, while he practiced the evil he didn't want to do. She swallowed. "That was low," she breathed.

"No, it's not," he disagreed, his voice gentle now. "I'm fighting for you, Liz." He grasped her arms and pulled her body against him, even as she strained away.

"Let me go," she demanded, wedging her hands between his chest and hers.

"I can't," he whispered, kissing her forehead. "I'm fighting for you, and I'll make you remember how it was between us. It's the only weapon I have." He kissed her nose.

The feel of his lips on her skin stirred the memories he spoke about. Her back started catching afire with sensations of a sexual vein—his hands on her like matches and her skin like sulfur.

"I miss your soft places, Liz, and the way only you can touch and ignite me. I miss the excitement and adventure of loving you. I crave the way you invented alternative ways to try familiar things."

More than her heart throbbed as his seductive words brought back erotic memories that they should never have made together. He kissed her mouth, deep and bold, the way she loved it, crushing her body against him as his lips pressed against hers, the force of the kiss telling the height of his need for her. Elizabeth felt the frayed fringes of her inner fight unravel like a ball of yarn tumbling downhill. *I shouldn't do this*. But the words echoed with a distant ring, possessing no strength to emit an objection or penetrate the passion rising in her soul from Terence's touch. One more time, she went with him somewhere that Exodus 20:14 called adultery.

***

It was a minute before midnight, and the warmth Terence had left behind drained away as recriminations set in. Elizabeth closed her eyes as tears burned them. What was the use of crying? She'd sinned one more time, had sex with a man who was another woman's husband, knowing all along that it was wrong. So why had she done it? Because it felt good and she loved him. His body against hers stirred a desire in her that made her crazy, built heat in her blood to a level from which there was no let down except that they made love. Since she knew it was wrong, why couldn't she exercise her will to say no? Was the illicit love worth it when she felt so terrible afterwards? For three weeks, she'd had peace because he hadn't come around, hadn't called her, and hadn't touched her. Yet, one meeting, a few touches, and some sweet words had turned her into a fornicator again. How could she ask forgiveness for something that wasn't a mistake? Elizabeth brushed tears from her cheeks. *Oh God, please help me. I want to stop this, but my flesh is sick and frail. Lend me Your strength, Jesus, please. In 2 Corinthians 12:9, You said Your "strength" is perfected in "weakness," Jesus. Oh God, I don't know that I can be any weaker or lower than I am now. Lift me up, Lord God, and fill me with Yourself so that I will have the strength to do what's right.*

But the very next day, right doing became a challenge once more for Elizabeth.

***

At eight o'clock the next morning, she lifted a hand that felt like lead and rang the bell of the small, white house on Meridian Drive on the east side of town. He'd moved to Mountain Spring, one of the four Seneca Mountain communities, a year ago and one year after she did.

Initially, she had thought he followed her here. He'd been after her since the tenth grade. Unfortunately, they had ended up in the same college. He seemed to take it as an auspicious omen that they were meant to be together. To Elizabeth, it had been bad luck. He was nice and meant well, so she never wanted to snub his overtures of friendship and his occasional expression that he was interested in them having a dating relationship. But when he turned up at her former church in Hempstead, New York, after being blessedly absent for ten years from her life, Elizabeth dispensed with civility and told him she'd never be interested in a man with a flaccid body like his and teeth tamed by braces at his advanced age. She had somebody, didn't want him, and never would—infamous last words.

Now here she was, on the doorstep of the man she'd said those awful words to and very much in need of him. *His help*, she amended in her head. As the lock turned, Elizabeth straightened her shoulders and lifted her head, trying to gather her melting self-confidence for what she was about to do.

Isaac Jones didn't even get a chance to tell her good morning, much less find out why she was on his doorstep at this time of the day. If his heart had been weak, he would have expired—her action was that shocking. Moist, warm, and sweet, her mouth covered his fast and moved over his lips at the same speed. In the back of his frozen mind, Isaac figured Elizabeth Monroe had kissed a man before. She didn't move like a novice, but like a woman who knew her way around a man's lips and knew the type of dance that ignited and elevated excitement. He didn't question her motive, didn't hazard if this were a moment of madness. Like any man, he made the most of this ride and thanked God for his good fortune.

Shock sprinted away, replaced by soaring desire for a woman he'd admired for nineteen years. He responded with passion to her ardent caress and felt her tiny pause of surprise at the heat of his kiss. But neither she nor he dwelt on the implication of that hesitation as they both indulged in an edgy, fire-hot, and completely new exploration of intimacy.

When they separated, the struggle for air was real. Labored breathing disturbed the morning air on a street not yet fully awake. Stay-at-home moms with pre-pre-school kids hadn't yet ventured outdoors, and husbands, most of whom, worked in New York City or Albany, were long gone. It was just them, the Langley's dog across the street, and the summer breeze drifting across front lawns and cooling their heated bodies.

"I wanted to say good morning. Are you free for dinner tonight?"

Her husky voice tiptoed down his spine like a soft wind, making him shiver with imagined pleasure. Isaac stared at the nearly six foot tall woman before him glad he could look directly into her eyes although she wore heels. Her eyes—dark brown pools of swirling chocolate—

mesmerized him. *Did she just ask me out?* he wondered tipsily. He opened his mouth and couldn't form one letter, much less words. She smiled and stole even his breath. Her beauty always left him bereft—of words, of sense, of everything, except how much he desired her. Ginger cookie brown skin shone, showcasing its moisturized perfection. Hair, shiny and black, tumbled in gentle waves to her shoulders. Lashes, thick and dark, swept up and down at a slight blink, and her trimmed-to-a-thin-line brows inched up her forehead at his silence. She smiled again, and Isaac helplessly followed the curve of her plump lips, trying to curb his craving for another taste of her.

"I'll take your silence for consent," she murmured, delving into her purse. "Here's my card." She tucked a business card into the pocket of his cotton dress shirt. "My cell's on the back. Call me."

Several seconds after her Acura pulled away from the curb, Isaac roused himself enough to close his front door and lean against it. After that incredible kiss, he wanted to know now more than ever what had motivated this three hundred and sixty degree turn in a woman who didn't mince words when she told him he was too skinny and his braces were repulsive. That was two years ago in Hempstead, but he'd been in this town, Mountain Spring, her town, for the past year and she hadn't given him the time of day.

They attended the same church, First Mountain Spring Second Advent Believers (SAB). Yet, she had barely answered him the times he tried to talk to her during the entire year he went there. When she passed him, it was as if he didn't exist. Something was up. Isaac was interested in Elizabeth Monroe enough to want to find out. One thing he was sure of, and it was that she hadn't fallen madly in love with him overnight. He wasn't as skinny as he was two years ago. A vigilant and arduous personal trainer at McBride's Best Body Gym had given him biceps that he hadn't believed possible and abs that made women at the gym do double takes. His braces were gone as well. But hadn't she noticed those things in the past year? Isaac doubted it was a sudden appreciation for his physique or the absence of wire on his teeth that motivated Elizabeth's sudden interest.

He pulled her business card from his pocket and looked at the number. The only way to discover her motive was to meet her later. She hadn't set the time. It would have to be late, around eight o'clock. He had a deadline for the architectural plans he was working on. Today was going to be long and not only because of his job project.

CHAPTER II

Elizabeth pulled over to the curb on the adjacent street and gripped the steering wheel, trying to still her trembling. Confusion, surprise, and concern bounced through her body like lottery balls popping out with winning numbers. She fervently hoped that she'd win in this game of pretense she played to gain her own advantage.

She needed a husband fast so that she could foist this pregnancy on him. Isaac Jones already liked her. That covered half the effort to the altar. The rest should be a breeze. All she had to do was work her wiles on him. He'd say 'I do' before he figured the answer should have been the opposite. Elizabeth's conscience pricked her. What she had in mind amounted to using a person. She ignored the guilty feeling. What other choice did she have? Besides, maybe it wouldn't be so bad marrying him with the way his kiss made her feel. The thrill of it had been unexpected. The racing of her pulse surprised her; the pounding of her heart frightened. Hadn't she experienced the same reactions with Terence Love only last night? He still had her heart, so how could Isaac Jones, a man she was far from attracted to, stir the same feelings within her? Maybe it was just a physical reaction. Maybe she was used to being kissed and her body automatically responded. All that sounded like baloney, and Elizabeth knew that it was.

Isaac knew how to make a kiss fulfilling, and the connection with him had satisfied her, which was what caused surprise. She hadn't expected that. For her, he held no facial appeal. Probably the fact that his braces were gone made a difference. But it wasn't that. She'd startled him with her unexpected action, but he'd recovered and participated. His kiss had been heady and enticing, sexy and stirring, and thorough and satisfying. Elizabeth wanted more. That was the scary part. How could she want more when only last night she'd given in to a craving for Terence?

Last night's surrender happened because she still yearned for him. Even after she'd ended their relationship mere hours ago, the second closure to their affair, she had relived in her head all their times together, especially what they'd done last night. Elizabeth shook her head hard to eject the thoughts surging back from that memory. *What are you doing, Liz? Stop it! Stop thinking about him or the intimacy. It'll only lead to more of the same.* She had done the right thing in sending him back home to his wife—a pity it was after and not before she'd succumbed to him.

When he originally ended their relationship, Elizabeth hadn't voiced an objection then. It would have been pointless. He was someone else's husband, and she was the other woman—something she never thought she would be, having not been raised that way. But one night and one mistake had turned into two years of error and indiscretion—that sounded better than sin. In her head, she was glad he'd ended it the first time, since she hadn't found the moral courage to do it. And in her head, she felt glad she had ended it again last night. In her heart, she hurt because she cared for him.

The time on the dashboard placed the hour at eight-twenty a.m. She had to deliver a lecture via videoconference in ten minutes. Elizabeth stepped on the gas, knowing she might have to run a few amber and probably some red lights to make it.

***

If he'd known three kids would have more than doubled her dress size, he would've stopped at one or maybe not impregnated her at all. Terence looked at his wife across the breakfast table, having put the last child on the bus, and tried to resize her from a twenty to an eight. It wasn't working. Sonja was still heavy and undesirable. It was his day off from Mountain Spring's emergency call center. Had he known she'd taken today off from her nursing job at the town's hospital, he'd have switched days with a co-worker. He'd broken up with Elizabeth after the final sermon of the family life series her brother-in-law, Pastor Douglas

11

Watson, had preached. He loved his kids and didn't want them scarred by parental separation. Continuing on the path he was on, stepping out on his wife, would make that end inevitable. So he'd quit cheating. Then he started going through withdrawal, wanting something that he could no longer have—the intimacy with Elizabeth, which was why he'd ended up sleeping with Liz last night. Intimacy was available at home, but he had no desire to get it from that quarter. He couldn't get in the mood; every look at Sonja killed any idea of that kind of proximity to her. She was still a pretty woman—cute like the day he married her, but he couldn't keep his eyes on her face through the whole lovemaking thing. And if his gaze dropped lower, his libido, what little there was of it around her, would lie down and die a fast death.

"I'm going to the gym," he announced. He could not stay here with her.

"Oh, may I come with you?" she asked, smiling at him.

"You want to come to the gym?" he asked, surprised.

"Why is that so shocking?"

Why are you amazed that I am surprised? Terence watched her push the kitchen table slightly away so she could get out of her chair. Why had she wedged herself there? He glanced away, especially so he wouldn't see her hips when she stood. She'd expanded there a lot. "You don't like walking. Going to the gym is more than that." He gave her a meaningful look. "Do you *really* want to go?"

Her gaze fell to the bills she'd been sorting on the table. "No, I don't really want to," she said softly. She glanced up and met his eyes. "But I really *need* to go."

He broke eye contact, feeling his heart shift with sympathy from the pleading look in her eyes. She knew she was heavy, had referenced it a few times, in particular, when he'd refused to make love to her. This was the first time she'd ever expressed a desire to do something about it, though. Terence didn't want her going to the gym with him. For one, most of the girls at the gym thought he was single, and he flirted when they did. They liked how he looked and he didn't mind their admiration. Sonja going with him would kill all that, but how could he refuse to take her? "Switch the jeans for some sweats, and we'll go," he told her.

She smiled as if his answer fulfilled her hope. "I'll be right back," she promised and hurried upstairs to change.

He glanced at his phone and scrolled through his contacts. His thumb hovered over one name beneath the letter 'm'. Should he call? For what purpose? It was over; he'd done the right thing the first time and ended it; she'd done the right thing last night by telling him not to come back. But desire was a heck of a thing, and getting the forbidden fruit from his taste buds was harder than he imagined it would be.

"I'm ready," Sonja announced as she returned to the kitchen.

Opportunity over. Terence hit the refresh button and switched to the home screen.

CHAPTER III

At five o'clock that evening, Elizabeth stood in the pick-up line at Shane's pharmacy waiting to get her prescription. The elderly woman at the counter was asking questions about her diabetes medication. The two people ahead of her in the line, two senior citizens, discussed the side effects of their high blood pressure meds and exchanged brand names. Elizabeth hoped she wouldn't get any side effects from her prescription. She'd read that iron rich supplements could cause stomach upset. With her stomach starting to feel queasy in the mornings, she didn't need anything else to unsettle it more. It was the queasiness that pushed her into the doctor's office. That plus her missed period, although she wasn't regular. After a two-week absence of her monthly unwelcome visitor, she'd gotten concerned. She'd skipped the home test and gone straight to the professional. So the positive was undeniable. She was nearly a month pregnant for a man she couldn't tell about her pregnancy.

"Hi, Sister Monroe."

Elizabeth glanced up from staring at the tiled floor and prayed that a sinkhole would appear and suck her out of the place. Mistletoe Roper! The teenager who sang on the praise team worked here? How much more unfortunate could she be? One church member knowing her business meant one too many. She was not filling that prescription today. "Hi, Mistletoe," she greeted the girl, forcing a smile. "Stockings," she muttered and snapped her fingers as if she'd just remembered. With that, she started a turn to allegedly get the item, even though she was really in pre-flight mode. That plan bit the dust with Mistletoe's next remark.

"Bring them to this counter. We can check them out with your prenatal vitamins."

Elizabeth froze for a second and then mobility returned, sending her down the hosiery aisle almost at a sprint. She grabbed the first store brand she saw and headed back to the pharmacy, shame and disgrace burning through her body and heating her skin. At the counter, she did not meet the girl's eyes. Elizabeth did not want to know what she was thinking. She swiped her card, grabbed her receipt, and muttered what she hoped was a pleasant good bye before marching with rapid steps out the exit doors.

She was not going back to First Mountain Spring SAB church, at least not until she got Isaac to the altar or the courthouse. It might have to be the latter with the urgency of her situation.

***

Isaac checked out his reflection in the full-length mirror of his armoire. He liked the guy looking back at him. He grinned at his image, spun around, and gave himself thumbs up. He looked good. Why had he waited so long to lift weights when the results were so confidence-enhancing? His starch-crisp white shirt fit his shoulders perfectly and slid down a chest and abdomen made rock hard by pounds he never thought he'd lift in his lifetime. Relaxed-fit deep blue jeans covered his legs, their tips resting on the tops of his dark tan Dockers. He grabbed his sport jacket and his keys and headed out the door bound for Elizabeth's house. Isaac was looking forward to the evening.

***

Elizabeth chose a sleeveless baby blue dress with fitted bodice and a flared skirt with boxed pleats. Her aim was a sweet and sexy effect, and her reflection indicated that she'd achieved the outcome. White ankle strap sandals and a white clutch purse rounded out her outfit. The doorbell rang. She sprayed perfume into the atmosphere and ran through the mist like she always did.

***

Her hair looked like she'd stepped right out of the salon. Wisps of it curled at her temples and three locks brushed the corner of her left eye. She had caught the rest of it in an upswept style with curls cascading

15

down like a polished waterfall of coiled black satin.

Isaac swallowed, trying to find saliva and his voice as his eyes drifted down her full chest, slid over her abdomen, past curvaceous hips to her knees and the skin showing above it.

"Should I change? Is the skirt too short?" she asked, worriedly, although she wasn't at all disturbed since she'd dressed to disturb him. Seemed like it was working.

The skirt was a little on the skimpy side, but Isaac liked the view and didn't want to lose it. "It's perfect, and you are beautiful," he complimented her. He cleared his throat. Nobody could call his voice husky, but he'd descended some decibels just now.

"Thank you, Isaac." Like this morning, she went seductive with her cadence and it affected him the same way—knocked his heart off beat, his senses off balance, and his coordination off sync. Several blinks and a breath rescued him, and he managed to offer her the flower he held behind his back.

"I wasn't sure if a rose would be too much, so I brought a carnation," he said, smiling a bit lamely.

Elizabeth accepted it and inhaled the gentle fragrance, feeling a quivery appreciation in her heart at his thoughtfulness. She fluttered her lashes at him, brushed the carnation against her lips, and then against his cheek, transferring the kiss that way. A slow smile crept across his lips, which meant he understood her salute. She stepped out of her apartment and locked the door.

Outside her building, Isaac led the way to a silver Ford Escape Sports Utility Vehicle. He opened her door, and she slid in, letting her purse fall to her feet–an accident from his perspective but a deliberate act on her part. As she hoped he would, Isaac bent to retrieve it, and Elizabeth copied his action, timing it so that their faces met at her knee.

"I can get it," she whispered, smiling into his walnut eyes.

When he kept staring, Elizabeth knew he was mesmerized, precisely how she wanted him to be, and he was where he should be. She capitalized on the moment she'd maneuvered and kissed him. Bold, blatant, unchaste, and sexual, she caressed his mouth with her own and pulled back before either of them received satiation—her intent to awaken his desire and leave it smoldering so that he could think of nothing else but her. She smiled; he blinked. She took her purse; he stepped back. She reached for her seatbelt; he closed the door.

***

He needed a moment. Isaac took it and took in lots of air at the back of his vehicle. *Steady, Isaac, steady*, he warned himself silently. She was a dream come true, but this all might be *too* good to be true. It was so incredible that it felt unreal. Would he wake up and find that Elizabeth Monroe, the woman he'd dreamed of his whole life, hadn't thoroughly kissed him twice in less than twelve hours? Before the night was out, he was going to go for a third and hope to the good Lord that he wouldn't strike out.

***

Isaac pulled out of East Meadows apartment complex where Elizabeth lived and headed down Starcrest Boulevard towards downtown Mountain Spring. He turned the music up on the a cappella CD, and Elizabeth automatically hummed along with the song "Lead Me to Rest" that she hadn't heard in ages.

They stopped at a traffic light, and she swung her head towards him in surprise at the husky rumble coming from his side of the car. He hummed the chorus in a low voice—definitely a tenor—and kept beat with the music. She hadn't known that he could sing. He was good.

He glanced her way with a slight smile. She returned it, noting at the back of her mind that the smile gave his face an appeal that it didn't naturally have. Everybody had a unique physical allure, she supposed, but she couldn't see his. The first time she kissed him, she had closed her eyes and braced herself because his face didn't stir a desire for her to be close to him. His kiss did that, though. Elizabeth wasn't sure if his ears turned her off him physically—the way they stood out at either side of his head like a bat spreading its wings to take a nocturnal journey. Or maybe it was the smallness of his eyes that seemed out of proportion with the other parts of his face, his very visible nose and full—she didn't want to use 'thick'—lips. She tried to find something positive in his features and decided that his neatly trimmed and low cut hair, along with his clean-shaven jaw—she didn't like the dark shadow that shaving left behind—made the sight of him a little easier. His body was still lean, but he was no longer skinny. Muscle was everywhere and a manly strength in his physique that, as a female, she could appreciate. The space that had been between his teeth years ago had disappeared. Braces achieved that, but Elizabeth was glad that he no longer wore them. She didn't think she would have kissed him if they were still on his teeth.

Isaac Jones wasn't what she wanted in a husband, at least not physically; however, she wasn't in a position to be picky. Elizabeth would take what she could get and hope for the best.

***

Selena's Mexican American restaurant was full tonight like every night. Isaac had called ahead and reserved a private booth for them.

"Spanish rice, chili, a garden salad, guacamole, and flan for dessert," Elizabeth said as soon as the waiter led them to their table and left them with menus.

"You didn't even look at the menu," Isaac countered, raising an eyebrow.

"I eat here a lot, so I know what I want." *And I want you.* Elizabeth had lots of practice with seduction. After all, she'd practiced on a man who belonged to somebody else, so she'd come up with quite a few tricks to keep him interested. She used them on Isaac now. Making her gaze sleepy and inviting, Elizabeth partially lowered her lashes and communicated the silent 'I want you' message in her head. At first, Isaac looked confused. Uncertainty edged into disbelief, and then nervousness set in. His eyes fell to his menu, and it took three tries for him to get it open. Elizabeth almost laughed, knowing he didn't have experience with handling a woman coming onto him, especially a woman he thought he could never have.

"Sample my choice," she suggested. "I taste good," she added deliberately, and then amended when his startled gaze flew to hers, "I have good taste, I mean."

She saw his Adam's apple rise and fall. Her plan was to have him fall into the trap she was setting for him. She imagined his mind was reeling with confusion and shock. To inject some stability into his equilibrium, she moved the conversation to something safe—drinks. "The watermelon agua fresca here is very good. Would you like to try it?"

"What's in it?"

"No alcohol," she reassured him.

He smiled. "I didn't think there would be since you're suggesting it."

Elizabeth could not resist. "And why do you think I suggest safe things…or do them for that matter?"

The innuendo registered, and he studied her speculatively. His eyes roamed over her face and dropped to the lace top of her dress, turning hungry at the glimpses of skin it revealed. "Yesterday I might have thought you were safe. Today, you're outright dangerous."

The husky timbre of his usually gentle voice built the seduction she'd injected into the air.

Elizabeth sipped water and sent him a mysterious smile. *You haven't seen dangerous yet.* "Why do you say that?" she asked, widening eyes, which were far from innocent.

He leaned forward and rested his elbows on the table. "I don't think you want to hear my answer."

"Oh, yes, I do," she countered.

"Okay, then, here goes. When you show up at a man's door early in the morning without even a greeting and knock him into another dimension with the kind of kiss that updates the meaning of lascivious—that's dangerous." He checked that first point off on a finger, and continued, "When you repeat that action a mere twelve hours later, that's edgy *and* dangerous." Another finger went up. "When you talk to me the way you've been talking, your tone threaded through with suggestiveness, that's almost sexier than I can bear and goes way beyond dangerous."

The waiter came, and he paused while the man took their drink and food orders.

"My question is," he went on when the guy left the booth and closed the door behind him, "are you always this bold?"

"Only when I want something badly," she admitted, watching him with an evocative gaze from beneath her lashes.

"Since when do you want me?"

From the bald and a bit bewildered question, Elizabeth could see that he needed convincing about the want part—as in her wanting him. Unlike in the general restaurant area with individual chairs, Selena's private cubicles had booth-upholstered seats. She switched from hers to his and dropped her hand to his thigh. "Since you developed muscles that make me yearn to touch you," she answered his question, sliding her hand in reverse up his thigh.

He halted her progress quickly. "Careful," he warned. "You can get yourself into a whole lot of trouble like this."

"I've played it safe all my thirty-five years. I think it's way past time to get risky."

"Why me?"

Didn't I just answer that? Maybe he wasn't satisfied with her first reply. "You already like me," she tried again. "I don't have to prove myself to you." Elizabeth told him some semblance of the truth, which really was that she needed a man who was already enamored with her since she had thirty days to marry him—no time to get him to fall for her. She hoped her belly wouldn't be showing by then.

He smiled; it wasn't humorous—more self-mocking. "So, *now* you want the skinny guy with wire on his teeth?"

Isaac Jones was nobody's fool. He knew she hadn't developed a sudden affinity for him, with the way she'd insulted and snubbed him in the past. Elizabeth committed to working harder at convincing him.

"I don't see you like that anymore," she confessed softly.

"Why? Because I got some muscle and lost my braces?"

"It's not that," Elizabeth answered, her voice lower than before.

"I'm the same man. I haven't changed. So, why're you interested?" He gave her a quizzical look.

Elizabeth thought about her pregnancy, the fact that she wasn't married, and the reality that she was a Christian, at least she claimed to be. She thought about her need for a husband, the fulfillment of which seemed to be slipping away with Isaac's guard going up, and she suddenly felt alone and overwhelmed. The tears she'd been trying to manufacture came easily now. A trail of liquid slid down one cheek and then tracked south down the other. She lowered her head so he wouldn't see, but he caught on when she sniffled and a tear landed on the white tablecloth.

"Liz?" Isaac shortened her name in the query.

"You want to know why I'm interested in you?" she whispered. "I'm tired—tired of charming and handsome men turning into toads. I'm tired of disappointments and getting hurt. I'm tired of making mistakes." That last bit was the truth. She'd made a huge mistake sleeping with a married man and an even bigger one getting pregnant for him.

Isaac eased his arm around her shoulders and tugged her against him. Elizabeth relaxed in his embrace and accepted the comfort he offered.

"Sometimes we have to wade through muck to find a miracle," he said, his quiet tone soothing. "Not that I'm suggesting I'm one—a miracle, that is."

She heard the smile in his voice. Elizabeth was hoping that he'd be her miracle. "I thought," she picked up where she'd left off, "maybe if I reached out for someone who already appreciated me, I wouldn't keep getting hurt by guys I valued more than they valued me." Technically, that only happened with Terence.

Silence followed her last words and stretched. Elizabeth wiped her eyes and nose. Had she gotten through to him? Did he empathize enough to stop being skeptical about her interest in him? With him saying nothing, it didn't seem like she had.

"I hear you," he finally said. "I need to get something straight, though."

Elizabeth pushed off his chest. "What?" she prompted.

"You sound like you don't want the work of learning to appreciate somebody's personality. Do you only want a man who wants you? Is that enough for you?"

It sounded terrible when he said it like that. Since she didn't want to confirm it, she asked instead, "Isn't it enough for you?"

"No, it's not." His quiet answer was fast and firm, as if the question needed no consideration.

Oh boy. Trouble on the horizon...maybe. "What are you looking for?"

"Why do you think I'm looking?" He raised an eyebrow in amusement.

He had a point. She'd made an assumption. Now Elizabeth made a decision, which she hoped would not backfire. "If you're not looking, then I'm wasting my time and yours."

He gave her a calculating look. "I want a woman who loves me like I love her."

Was he in love with her? But he couldn't be. She hadn't spoken to him in a while, and they had never even dated. Tonight was their first one. Elizabeth ran her tongue around her lips and met the seriousness in his eyes. "What are you saying?" she asked him.

"A relationship is a two-way street, Elizabeth—giving and receiving," he said soberly. "A one-sided affection creates a lot of unhappiness. I'd rather be alone than be with someone who doesn't really feel anything for me."

"You think I don't feel anything for you?"

"You tell me. Do you?"

How could she answer the question honestly?

CHAPTER IV

The waiter delivered the meal, and she waited until Isaac had prayed before answering. "Would I have kissed you the way I had if I didn't feel anything?"

He held her gaze for a long time before finally saying, "No, I don't think so."

Heady relief rose in her heart. Elizabeth turned her attention to her plate, popped a forkful of guacamole into her mouth, and fought to keep the avocado dish from coming up the moment it hit her stomach.

"Liz?" Isaac used the shortened form of her name for the second time that night. "Are you all right?"

She closed her eyes, clenched her teeth, and begged God not to let her food come up. Her body grew warm with her effort to stem the reversal, and she shuddered as the nausea subsided and the food stayed down. Maybe she shouldn't eat anything more. Definitely, there would be no more guacamole for her tonight.

"Liz, maybe we should go," Isaac suggested with concern.

She opened her eyes to see that he'd risen halfway out of his seat and was watching her with a worried expression. Elizabeth managed a smile. "Sit down, Isaac." She waved him back into his seat. "I'm all right."

"Maybe you shouldn't eat anymore guacamole," he suggested.

He knew her stomach was upset, which made him a very observant man. It would behoove her to remember that. "Maybe not," she agreed and took a tentative taste of the rice. It stayed down, and she took another mixed with a bit of chili.

"What are you doing with yourself these days?" he asked conversationally.

Did he want personal or professional details? She went with professional since it was safer. "I teach undergraduate courses in English and U.S. History online. I'm a distance-learning professor with two universities, and I do some editing on the side, as well."

"You majored in English, as I remember. Right?" He pushed the guacamole aside and worked on his salad.

Feeling guilty, she started working on hers. She was more of a fruit rather than lettuce girl for roughage. "I did, and then ended up with two masters: an MFA in Creative Writing and a masters degree in History."

"You always liked writing. Are you still inventing short stories?"

"I haven't made up anything in a while." She shook her head and pulled a rueful face. "These days I teach the skill rather than practice it. I'm so busy that I don't have much time to write."

"You should start again. You're very good."

"I shared one story with you. Do you even remember it?" she quizzed, searching his face.

"I remember it was a humorous yet sobering tale of what transpires in the church from the eyes of a pastor's kid."

She'd shared a bit of that story with him in college. Elizabeth was surprised that he remembered after so many years. Warmth built in her heart towards him. "Speaking of creativity, isn't that what you do, too, only with buildings in contrast to my words. You're an architect with a respected firm in this area. You're with Structures and Designs, over on Main Street, correct?"

He looked surprised that she had that much detail about him. "I didn't think you were aware I existed, much less knew where I worked," he told her frankly.

Elizabeth felt a little badly. She had not been nice to him and had deliberately ignored him since he came to Mountain Spring and to her church. Only yesterday, she'd found out where he worked, since she had plans to get acquainted. She kept that detail to herself. Making a chiding sound, she murmured, "When a girl is interested in a guy, the way I am in you, she checks into little details."

"Like whether he has a job and can pay for this meal," he joked.

"I can pay for dinner, since I issued the invitation." Elizabeth smiled, but underneath she was serious.

He waved that away. "I wouldn't let you do that."

"It's the twenty-first century. Women pick up tabs or split them."

"I'm in the century but not in all respects—I'll pick up the tab."

Elizabeth smiled. "I won't fight you on that, but I'm a little concerned."

"About what?"

"About the things you are pre-twenty-first century on."

"Can I be honest with you?"

Should she even answer that with her deceit? "Go ahead."

"I prefer to chase a girl rather than have her come after me."

Uh, oh. Is he sending me a veiled message? Time wasn't on her side, so clearing confusion from the outset was best. "I'm surprised you came on this date then."

"Why is that?"

"I asked you out. With your way of thinking, that constitutes me chasing you."

"Technically, you didn't ask me out."

Her eyebrows inched upwards. "My recollection is different."

"You asked if I was free. You didn't invite me to anything."

Elizabeth thought his reasoning was skewed, but she didn't say that. "So that's why you're here. You wouldn't have come otherwise?"

"I would have. I always make an exception for you, Liz." He smiled and turned his attention back to his plate.

The simple comment created a funny little twist in her heart. No frills or fancy words, just the truth. That awareness roused her slumbering conscience and Elizabeth felt wretched that she wasn't being truthful with him. Her eyes fell to her plate without interest—her lack of enthusiasm motivated by much more than fear of queasiness. Isaac Jones was a good man and a nice guy. He didn't deserve what she was trying to do to him. Yet, with no other prospects on the horizon, what alternative did she have?

CHAPTER V

"Elizabeth Monroe is pregnant?"

Terence stopped short outside Azalea's door. *Elizabeth is pregnant!* Stunned, he stared at his teenaged daughter's bedroom door. *Why didn't she tell me?*

"How do you know this?" he heard her ask whoever was on the line with her.

"She picked up a pre-natal prescription at the pharmacy?" she echoed in a tone riddled with disbelief. "Maybe she got it for somebody else."

Terence held his breath in the pause following that. "I'm not stupid, Mistletoe," his daughter declared, sounding miffed at her friend apparently giving her that label. "She *could* have picked it up for somebody else. I didn't know her name was on the prescription. It's hard to believe that she's pregnant." She paused again, and then said, "Why? Well, because she's the pastor's sister-in-law and I heard her father was a minister. You'd think that with so much holiness in her family, she'd be holy, too. Don't tell anybody?" Azalea asked Mistletoe the question as if she felt offended that the girl doubted her ability to be discreet.

Terence thought it ironic that the gossiper wanted to maintain a secret that she'd already blown wide open. He stepped away from the door, intent on finding some privacy to call Elizabeth. As if that was likely in a house where there was not much of it with three daughters and a wife all at home when he wanted to call his ex-mistress.

***

The warm summer night, its balmy breeze, and the shadows cast by trees along the concrete walk to her building suffused the air with a romantic intimacy that called for closeness between couples and lingering kisses along the way. Elizabeth figured Isaac wasn't feeling it since he walked beside her with his hands in his pockets, the perfect escort and the perfect gentleman. It wasn't what she wanted him to be, and a polite 'good night' wasn't the way she wanted the evening to end. He preferred to chase, but his pace wasn't in sync with hers; he seemed in the slow and steady mood where a romance between them was concerned. She was on the fast and desperate track.

Elizabeth reasoned that in thirty days, her stomach wouldn't be noticeable enough for anybody to be suspicious. Anything beyond that and she'd be courting discovery. In the two-month pregnancies she'd viewed online, the women looked a bit bloated, kind of like they had pre-menstrual swelling of the abdomen. To be sure, she could ask her older sisters, Karen and Adrianna, who between them had five kids. After five pregnancies, they should have a pretty accurate idea of when a woman started showing. Elizabeth ditched the idea because they would want to know why she was asking, which would require more lying. At the rate she was going, she would turn into the pathological kind before long.

"Do you have a key?"

Isaac's question pulled her from her thoughts, and she got the keys and opened the main door of her apartment building. He followed her up the two flights of steps to her front door. She lifted the key but didn't insert it into the lock. He may prefer to make the moves, but she had no time to wait on him. Elizabeth glanced up, "Would you like to come in?"

He held her gaze with a steady one and a tiny smile. "For what?"

She drew a blank, taken aback by his answer. A man's usual answer would be 'yes.' Terence's replies to that offer had always been

27

affirmative. He was not Terence; she would do well to remember that. Elizabeth moistened her lips and laughed a little, nervous all of a sudden. "I'm not exactly sure."

He grinned. "Okay, then. I'll come in, and we can figure it out together."

"Okay," she agreed, even more off balance. What he just said hadn't been expected either.

Inside her apartment, she flipped the switch on and flooded her living room with light. Her leather sofa, wine red—almost burgundy— sat against the wall separating the room from the kitchen. Two ivory armchairs sat at right angles to the sofa. Altogether, the three chairs formed a semi-circle around the cottage coffee table, its color a mixture of the furniture hues.

"Have a seat," she invited, moving her hand in an arc that he could sit anywhere. "Oh, don't do that," she stopped him as he started easing out of his shoes. She had hardwood, not carpeting, so he didn't need to remove his Dockers.

"Habit," he said, bending and running a finger around the heel of the shoe as he forced his right foot back inside.

"Would you like something to drink?" she offered as he sat in one of the armchairs.

"No thanks, Liz." He shook his head. "Why don't you have a seat?" He smiled up at her. "We can talk a bit."

An impish thought entered her head. Elizabeth perched herself on one arm of his chair and arched an eyebrow at him.

His smile was slow and full of the playfulness in her action. "You got me on that one. I should have specified where," he said.

"And since you didn't, how about I sit here?" She eased onto his lap.

He didn't do or say anything. Isaac simply studied her the way he'd been doing all night, as if he were trying to figure her out. Elizabeth hoped to keep him guessing until she got him to say 'I do.' If he found her mysterious, that wasn't a bad thing. A bit of mystery always fed a man's interest.

"What are you doing, Liz?" he finally asked.

"I didn't give you permission to call me that," she objected, evading an answer.

"Then you should have let me know you didn't like it the first time I used it."

"I didn't say I didn't like it."

"So what's the problem?"

"Nothing. I kind of like the way you say it." She smiled and leaned against him, letting her hand creep up his chest to the second button of his shirt. With no effort, she slipped it from the hole. She was on the third one before he said something.

"Again, what are you doing?" The question was tense this time, and Elizabeth got the sense from the stiffening of his muscles beneath her derriere that the intimacy of her action was stirring awareness in him. This guy still wanted her. Elizabeth had no qualms about using his desire to trap him.

She ignored his question again and asked one of her own. "How long have you wanted me, Isaac?"

"What kind of question is that?" He sounded like he was at sea now.

"A pretty straightforward one. How long?"

"Ever since I met you."

"Which would make it almost twenty years."

He kept silent.

"I think," she said, pressing a kiss to the exposed skin at the neckline of his undershirt and smiling when he shivered, "that if you waited that long for a woman, and she came to her senses and wanted you back, you'd quit asking questions and start taking action."

"What action is that?" he asked, his voice strangled as she shifted on his lap in a deliberate way to sensitize him even more.

Elizabeth kissed his chest again, and wiggled her hand beneath the end of his shirt that she'd pulled from his jeans, splaying her palm against a solid abdomen that called her to explore its tautness. "You don't like women who chase you like I'm doing now, so I'm a little afraid to answer. I don't want to lose you. Promise me I won't."

"Won't what?" he asked, his breathing starting to sound like he was hiking up a mountain.

"Lose you."

"You won't," he managed, obviously trying to catch his breath as her hand climbed up his stomach, the tips of her fingers, caressing and stirring as she moved.

"Okay, here's my answer: The action is marriage."

He went very still. Elizabeth wondered if she'd been too bold, but what was she to do?

"You want to marry me?" The question denied an affirmative answer before she gave it.

"That would be correct," she said softly, closing her eyes and bussing his lips.

"Liz, we've only been on one date," he pointed out, sounding like he was in a surreal situation.

It felt a little fantastic to her too, but that usually happened when a girl did the unmentionable like propose after one date. "But we've shared two very hot and satisfying kisses," she countered and kissed him again, adding more intensity this time.

"Liz, we don't know each other enough to make a lifetime commitment."

She *had* to make a lifetime commitment, notwithstanding. "If this were my last night on earth and I proposed to you, you'd marry me, wouldn't you?"

He stiffened. "Is it your last?" he asked sounding like he believed it was.

"You didn't answer my question," she reminded him softly, continuing to kiss him.

He let her and then eased away to answer. "You make it hard for me to think," he muttered.

That's the idea. Don't consider, just commit to marrying me. "Would you?" she prodded gently.

"I would," he admitted.

"And you wouldn't have gotten time to know me. So what's the difference if you make a commitment now, even though I'm not dying tonight?"

He sighed. "The difference is time, Elizabeth, and we have time so why rush?"

"Will time change who I am or who you are?"

He frowned. "No, I guess not."

"Then we don't need to waste time waiting." She pushed off his chest and trained an earnest gaze on him, prepared to make her case.

"We share the most important things: we're educated, we're independent, we share religious beliefs, we..." she trailed off, running out of commonalities.

"We don't know enough about each other, Elizabeth," he repeated. "You ran out of steam before you even got started listing things we share in common. That should tell you we have a lot of work to do."

"I liked Liz better."

"I'm sorry."

"You started calling me Elizabeth. I prefer Liz."

"I called you that when we were in the tenth grade and you went off on me."

Elizabeth smiled. "That was a long time ago. I've changed a lot since then."

"That's the truth," he acknowledged dryly. "*Now* you want me."

She narrowed her eyes at him. "Don't get sarcastic with me," she snipped.

"I'm sarcastic when I tell the truth?"

"It's not the telling, it's the tone," she said, *her* tone conveying an attitude of its own.

He laughed and wrapped his arms around her. "I like the fire in you, Liz."

She smiled. "Thank you. I'll try to be more feisty in the future."

"I like sweet things," he said suddenly.

"Huh?" She was a little lost at the conversational shift.

He hugged her closer. "I like pancakes and doughnuts, apple pie and pumpkin pie. I like pineapple upside down cake and peanut butter cookies."

"How do you stay slim?"

"I said I like them. I don't eat them all the time, and, of course, I exercise."

"God just blessed some people to be lean."

"And He gave others some nice curves," he complimented her, pressing his palm against her waist.

Her pulse raced at the fast and silly thought that he could tell she was expecting by touching her there.

"I forget and leave the toilet seat up at times. I'm going to make a conscious effort to put the seat down from now on. I don't like to cook and I don't like to clean, but I do it because I hate being hungry, don't like going to restaurants all the time, and I don't like living in a mess."

"I hate laundry," she admitted.

"I'm good with that, and I like being neat so I don't mind the ironing."

"I'll cook and clean, if you do the laundry," she offered.

"Deal," he agreed.

Elizabeth knew her hope would come to fruition with that one word. They were getting to know each other, and he'd started them down this path, which meant marriage was more than on his mind. It was his endgame as much as hers. *Thank you, God.*

CHAPTER VI

Isaac hit the gym at five-thirty the following morning and was on a rower, simultaneously working his arms and legs when Terence Love showed up and climbed onto the machine beside him.

"Hey," Terence greeted.

Isaac slid forwards and then backwards on the rower, pacing his breathing, and greeted the other man quickly, "Morning."

Out of the corner of his eye, he saw Terence start his workout. Isaac kept going, building speed as his breathing allowed and feeling the burn in his arms and legs as he approached maximum endurance. Ten more slides and he was done. He lifted the towel from around his neck and mopped at the perspiration running down his temples. He had to lift some weights and then he'd be done for the day. On a Wednesday like today, he usually worked out with his personal trainer, Gary. The man was away at a conference. Isaac didn't want a substitute, so Gary planned to give him an extra training day next week. He swung his right leg to the left and got off the rower.

"You're done?" Terence asked.

Isaac glanced at the man whom he'd become friends with from their gym workouts. They both went to First Mountain Spring SAB Church, but he'd gotten to know Terence at McBride's Best Body Gym. They usually worked out at the same time in the mornings. Through the similarity of their gym routines, they'd gotten to know one another. Isaac knew he was married with three girls, knew that he'd wanted a boy but was thankful that his six, nine, and fourteen-year-olds were healthy.

33

Terence had also told him that things were a bit rocky with the wife. They'd met on Sunday mornings to shoot some hoops at the local park quite a few times. One of those times, Terence had confessed to an affair and worried that his wife and kids would find out and that he'd lose his kids. He planned to quit it. Isaac didn't know if he did. He'd even been surprised that Terence confessed something so private to him, but the older man had said that he had an aura about him that inspired a person to place confidence in him. Isaac had felt humbled. The man never brought the subject of his infidelity up again, and Isaac didn't pry. "I'm going to pump some iron, and then I'll be done," he answered. "What about you?"

"Same thing, but let me go with you to the weight room. I wanted to run something by you."

"Sure, let's go," Isaac agreed, glancing at Terence and noticing the strain in his face.

In the weight room, Isaac got to work with the dumbbells before going on to the barbells. Terence did the same. After about three half-hearted attempts, he set the dumbbells aside and with a sigh, rotated his neck and rolled his shoulders.

Isaac stopped his routine. "What's on your mind?" he asked, giving him an opening. He read the turmoil in the man's features when Terence raised his head.

"Remember how I told you about that affair," he started, pitching his voice low on the last word.

"I remember."

"Well, I think she's pregnant."

Isaac's eyes widened and he whistled. "Oh, man. I'm sorry to hear that. What do you plan to do?"

Terence lifted his shoulders helplessly. "I don't know. She won't take my calls."

Isaac's brows folded. "You had a quarrel?"

"No, we ended it. We're not seeing each other anymore."

"Because she's pregnant?" Isaac didn't understand.

He shook his head. "No, I just found that out. I've been trying to call her since last night, but her phone keeps going to voicemail."

"Why don't you go by her house?"

"I tried that. She doesn't answer the door," he confessed, running his hand over his head in frustration.

"Maybe she's angry you ended things and doesn't want to talk to you."

He shook his head. "It's not that. She understood I ended it to save my marriage and told me she was glad I did it because she'd already been feeling bad about the whole thing."

"Send her a text or an email," he suggested, not really knowing what to tell Terence.

"Do you think she'll answer?"

The guy seemed like he was clutching at straws and seeking an encouraging answer to keep his hope up.

"Nothing tried, nothing gained," Isaac said. It was the best he could do. He didn't know the reason for the woman's silence and didn't want to give Terence false hope.

"I'll do that. It's a good idea." Terence nodded and began to smile. "Look, man. I'm sorry to burden you with my problem, but I had to talk to somebody."

"It's no problem. I hope things work out. What do you plan to do, though, if it turns out that she's really pregnant?"

Terence sighed. "I don't know. If she is, I'll have to do right by her."

"It might hurt your marriage, something you'd been trying to avoid," Isaac reminded him with reluctance.

"I know." He sighed again and massaged his neck as if it hurt. "What would you do if you were in my shoes?" he asked, surprising Isaac.

He hoped he never found himself in Terence's predicament. When he married a woman, he planned to stay faithful to her. He'd never been a guy with a wandering eye.

"I hope I'm never in your shoes," Isaac told him honestly. "Especially since I'm thinking of getting married in the near future, but I—"

"You met someone?" Terence asked curiously.

Isaac smiled. "I did. Life's strange. She's a girl I knew in high school who would step over me if I tripped and fell in front of her. Now, she's interested."

"Maybe her biological clock is ticking," Terence snorted.

"Liz is only thirty-five. I don't think it's that. According to her, she's changed her outlook on life and what she wants in a man. She got burned enough times to wake up and get a good thing before it goes, meaning me. At least, she said something to that effect." He grinned.

"I'm glad for you, Isaac," Terence said, his smile genuine. "You're a good guy. You deserve a great girl."

"Thanks. Now back to what you asked me. If I were you, once I verified that the lady was pregnant, I'd tell my wife about my mistake. That's a tough thing that can have serious fallout, but I don't think there's any option. Your wife will find out anyway. You just don't want her to do that by accident. The consequences will be worse and the situation unsalvageable if you don't tell her."

Terence started grimacing halfway through his advice. "I'd rather not tell Sonja."

Isaac shrugged. "My advice is that you do, once you confirm that the lady is pregnant, but the ultimate decision is yours." Isaac glanced at his watch. There was no time for barbells. He'd do that tomorrow. "I wish you all the best, Terence. I'll see you tomorrow, by God's grace." He clapped the man on the shoulder and headed home to take a shower.

Terence tracked Isaac Jones's exit from the gym, turning over the man's advice in his head. The idea of talking to Sonja about his infidelity was forbidding. As much as sexual interest in his wife had died, he didn't want divorce to end his relationship with his kids. Sonja was an even-tempered and patient woman, but Terence doubted she'd tolerate his unfaithfulness. The possibility existed that she'd forgive him in time, since he was no longer cheating, but it would harm the marriage. Despite his physical disinterest in her, Terence didn't mind being married to her. She was a good mother and an excellent homemaker. He just wished she'd lose the weight. He wasn't asking her to return to the dress size she was when he first met her, but somewhere close would be nice. If she could get to Elizabeth's size, maybe he'd find her desirable again and wouldn't crave companionship with Liz. Terence stiffened all of a sudden as something Isaac said came back to him. He'd said his girlfriend's name was Liz and that she was thirty-five years old. Elizabeth's nickname was Liz and *she* was thirty-five. Had he and Isaac unwittingly been discussing the same woman? Lord Jesus! He covered his mouth as a massive and awful thought stung him like a hornet. Isaac said he was getting married in the near future to Liz, a girl who previously couldn't stand him and suddenly wanted him now. If it was the same Elizabeth, it meant that she was rushing into marriage with this man to cover up the pregnancy. The thought searing his brain like a branding iron, he fled the gym and headed for Elizabeth Monroe's apartment before six o'clock in the morning.

CHAPTER VII

Elizabeth ignored the doorbell, the same way she'd ignored the numerous phone calls, voicemails, and text messages. It was six-thirty in the morning. Terence had already sent her two texts and left her three voicemails. He was the only person who could be at her door at this unholy hour. His voicemails had been as terse as his text messages: *Are you pregnant?* If he knew, that meant Mistletoe Roper's lips had been flapping. At this point, she didn't worry about the church members finding out. Her business becoming theirs was inevitable. Her fear was in Isaac finding out. No matter how much he liked her, Elizabeth didn't think he'd take on another man's pregnancy. She thought about praying, but how could she ask God to aid and abet her in lying and duplicity? She needed to keep Isaac away from church and the church members, at least until he married her. There were four communities in the Seneca Mountain Area: Mountain Spring, Mohawk Valley, Indian Run, and Heart Haven. Each town had an SAB church. She had thirty days and four church days. She'd go to the Mohawk Valley church for two Sabbaths, and spend the remaining two Saturdays in Indian Run and Heart Haven.

When her doorbell rang again, she lost patience, grabbed her phone and answered Terence's text. To his 'Are you pregnant?' question, she replied: *DON'T bother me OR ELSE I'll tell Sonja the truth.* He never called or texted back.

***

The sun, which had been struggling all morning to come out, surrendered to the rain clouds, making the day dark and dreary. The sky opened up, and a driving, pelting rain pounded the roof of Elizabeth's Acura. It wasn't the best day to meet her sisters for their weekly Wednesday brunch in downtown Mountain Spring. She crawled down New Street, seeking a meter on street parking in vain. Every one was taken. No doubt, with the current downpour, everybody wanted proximity to the shops. She made a right into the three-hour municipal parking and found a space on the far side of the lot, closer to Green rather than New Street. Resigned to walking in the rain, she opened her umbrella and stepped out of the car. Glad that she'd ditched her sandals for sneakers instead, Elizabeth hopped over puddles, dodged between cars, and hurried towards Connie's Café, where she and her sisters had agreed to meet.

At ten-thirty on Wednesday morning, Connie's still had a good crowd. Adrianna, the eldest of the three of them, sat in the rear of the café. She was talking on the phone. Karen, her other sister, the one married to the pastor for First Mountain Spring SAB, Douglas, sat across from Dri, tapping the screen of her phone.

Adrianna saw her first and waved her over. "Hey, baby girl," she greeted, rising and hugging Elizabeth. She hugged her back, and then hugged Karen, who had stood as well. She pulled up a chair and sat, noticing that both girls had big cups of iced tea already and each had a sandwich. "Didn't you order for me?" she reproved teasingly.

Karen shook her head. "We didn't know what you wanted? Besides, you almost brought up what I ordered for you last week. Are you over that stomach virus?"

No, not for another nine months. "Yeah," she lied. *This habit becomes easier with practice,* Liz thought glumly. "Who's watching the kids?" she asked, not wanting to talk about stomach trouble when she wasn't sure if anything she ordered would stay down. Maybe she should fast, but that would raise questions.

"Douglas is for four hours," Karen answered.

"He's watching all five kids by himself?" Elizabeth asked, surprised.

"Don't underestimate my husband," Karen warned playfully. "He's very competent and versatile."

"Until you get back and find a child wrapped in toilet paper, another one soaked through with toilet water, and one missing," Elizabeth said dryly.

They all laughed. It had happened to Douglas before.

"Give him a break," Karen smiled. "It was one time."

"Aisha was the one who went missing. She was in the coat closet, playing hide and seek by herself," Dri said, grinning at the memory.

According to how they had told it to her, Douglas had truly been frantic, thinking that the child had opened the door and wandered off.

"Esther is a big help to him," Karen said proudly of her oldest child. "She helps him supervise her siblings and cousins."

At seven, Esther was the oldest of the children. Which made the others how old? Elizabeth couldn't keep up with the ages of all the kids. "How old are Jonah and Jared?" she asked Karen about her two boys.

"Jonah's five and Jared is three like Aisha," Karen told her.

"And Benjamin turned one last month, right?" she asked Adrianna about her son.

"He did," Dri answered. "Don't feel badly. It's hard to remember the DOBs of all the kids," she comforted Elizabeth.

"And it will only get more complicated when yours come along and the numbers go higher," Karen laughed.

"Speaking about that, it looks like you'll be adding little ones to the clan soon," Dri remarked, shooting suggestive glances at her.

Elizabeth almost choked on saliva as fear tried to outrun panic. How did Dri know about her pregnancy? Her sister spoke before she could ask.

"Christopher and I saw you and Isaac in Selena's last night."

"You did?" Elizabeth asked, going weak with relief. She hadn't seen Dri and her husband. "Where were you? I didn't see you."

"Not in a *private* booth like you and Isaac," Dri stressed, giving her a meaningful look. "Which is why I'm thinking this might be serious and that you'll be adding some cousins to our brood."

"It was just dinner," Elizabeth said lamely.

"I thought you didn't like him," Karen inserted with a frown. "You've practically ignored him the whole year he's been at church, barely answering his greetings sometimes and downright not doing so other times."

Elizabeth stared at the burgundy tablecloth and wondered why her sister had to be so observant.

"When did dislike turn into dating?" Karen asked.

Elizabeth swung a glance between her sisters. Both of them watched her with interest. "It was only dinner," she offered, trying again to downplay it.

"In a private booth," Dri reminded her.

"When did you two start dating?" Karen pressed.

Elizabeth wasn't offended by their curiosity. They were her sisters, and they had been asking her since she moved to Mountain Spring if there was a man in her life.

"It was our first one," she explained.

"No more gap in his teeth. That's a good thing," Dri teased, her eyes twinkling. Both women knew of her previous objection to Isaac.

"You've got muscle to hold onto now," Karen ribbed.

"Give me a little credit, girls. There's more to appreciate in a man than muscle."

"But it only helps his appeal," Karen insisted and Dri agreed, probably because both their husbands were fine like that.

"He likes me, so I thought why not," Elizabeth confessed a half-truth, more like a quarter, or nothing resembling the truth. *I'm pregnant and I need a husband.* That *was* the truth. "I'm not getting younger, and there's no line of testosterone-filled and fine specimens at my door."

"You're settling for what you can get?" Dri frowned at her.

Pretty much. "Not really. He's nice."

"Translation: Settling. It's not going to work if he doesn't appeal in some way, Liz," Karen warned gently.

Silence settled over their small group, and the waiter came and took Liz's order. She took an iced tea and a bagel. That should stay down. Her sisters were watching her expectantly. What could she say? She didn't dislike him, at least not like before. He was okay. Her heart didn't race when he was around, but she didn't find him repulsive—not

41

precisely. It was easier to kiss him with her eyes closed, but people closed their eyes during a kiss anyway. Elizabeth snapped her fingers mentally. She could share that positive with her sisters. "He's an awesome kisser."

Her sisters squealed and piped down a bit when people started casting looks their way.

"What else?" Dri asked.

Elizabeth lifted a shoulder. "He's good with laundry."

"You've been discussing the domestic?" Karen's eyebrows almost touched her low hairline.

Elizabeth's brows wrinkled. "We shouldn't?"

"No, baby, it means that this is serious," Dri said with a huge grin. *You'd better believe it is.*

"Would you mind having him as a brother-in-law?" she asked them.

"Is it *that* serious?" Karen widened her eyes in doubt. "I mean it's only been one date."

"And many kisses," Elizabeth added.

Adrianna started coughing. "How long have you been talking? It must be a while if you've been intimate like that."

With the kind of intimacy she'd been involved in, kissing was mild in comparison. "Less than twenty-four hours," Elizabeth answered Dri's question. She might as well start shocking them now. They had more in store, especially with the bullet-fast marriage she had planned.

"This is serious," Karen declared. "Do you love him, Liz?"

"No." She could not lie about that. "But that will come." She hoped so.

Both her sisters regarded her with skepticism.

"Liz, is there something you're not telling us?" Dri asked.

"Like what?" Elizabeth asked on guard, holding her breath and hoping her sisters weren't figuring out the truth.

"Like maybe you slept with him and have to cover up a problem."

"I didn't sleep with him, so there's no problem to cover up." She quibbled again with halftruths. There *was* a problem, just not one created with him.

"Liz, you're our baby sister," Karen said. "We're happily married, and we want the same for you. That won't happen unless you're with the right man—a man whom you love."

"It's not like I'm marrying him today. As I get to know him better, love will come."

"That's the second time you said that. It sounds like you're trying to convince yourself," Karen observed, giving her a searching look.

"I'm not; I know what I want, and I want Isaac," she answered her sister a bit harshly, irritated with her doubts.

"Okay, you don't have to get an attitude," Karen said, her voice turning chilly. "I just want what's best for you."

"Thanks, I know, and I appreciate it, sis." Elizabeth sent her a fond smile, which Karen returned.

"So, what movie are we seeing today?" Adrianna asked, changing the subject.

Elizabeth ate her bagel while they decided what to watch at the local cinema.

CHAPTER VIII

Seven Weeks Later

"That means I'm still infertile."

"I'm afraid so," Dr. Carrington confirmed with a sympathetic expression. "On the bright side," he added in an attempt at encouragement, "the sperm count is higher than the last time you were here."

"Just not high enough to impregnate a woman."

The doctor shook his head, regret written across his face that he had to be the bearer of bad news. Again, he tried to look on the bright side. "The fact that it's higher is a good sign, though. It means that it's climbing."

"Doc, the last time I had this checked was five years ago. If the count only went up that insignificantly," he flicked his finger against the sheet Dr. Carrington had given to him, "it'll take another ten years for me to father a child. I'll be forty-six years old by then."

"Forty-six these days is not old," Dr. Carrington said with a smile. "The body is 'fearfully' and 'wonderfully' made like the Bible tells us in Psalm 139:14. Have a little faith, Isaac. God still works miracles."

Isaac Jones huffed out a low laugh. Sure God worked miracles. It was belief in a miracle that had driven him to get his sperm count checked and that had him seated before the doctor this Wednesday morning when he should have been at work. Only, the miracle he'd

44

hoped for turned into disappointment and the sure knowledge that he'd been duped into a marriage. His wife was pregnant all right—just not for him, which likely meant Elizabeth had come to him already pregnant. Now he understood her sudden interest in him and her need for the rushed courtship. His mouth twisted into a bitter smile full of self-recriminations. He'd been infatuated with her for so many years that when she deigned to bless him with her attention, he hadn't looked too hard for plausible reasons for her interest. She'd lied about everything—about her reason for wanting him, about loving him, about the whole change of heart thing.

Little things, tiny oddities started rushing to his mind. Liz always closed her eyes when he came in close for a kiss. Did that mean she didn't find him appealing or was she imagining the man she was pregnant for? And who was that? Was the guy somebody from Mountain Spring or some place else? He thought about how she insisted on making love in the dark. Why was that? So that she didn't have to look at him during intercourse? Did she even enjoy their intimacy? And with the lies she'd told, was she truly climaxing when they were together or was she faking it? How could a man know the difference? He'd only ever been with one other woman, and he hadn't even known then.

"Isaac? Isaac?"

He heard Dr. Carrington calling him from far away. He shook off the discouraging thoughts but couldn't evict the despondency from his heart. He met the doctor's slightly sad gaze and pulled himself together. He didn't want any sympathy. He had enough to dose himself with. Isaac forced a smile. "Yeah, doc."

"Come back to see me in a month. Here, I want you to get these brands of vitamin c and zinc. They are higher milligrams than what you are taking."

He accepted the small sheet of paper the doctor handed to him, disinterested in anything to do with raising sperm count. What was the point? He didn't plan to make love to Elizabeth again.

"I know this isn't the result you'd hoped for Isaac, and I am sorry, but unlike many of my other patients with your condition, you know God, and that makes all the difference."

Did it? God hadn't given him the insight into Elizabeth's lying and stopped him from marrying her. Or had He and he'd ignored the clues?

Isaac didn't answer that, knowing where the blame would fall if he did and not yet ready to claim his mistake.

"Let me pray with you before you go," Dr. Carrington offered, rising from his chair and coming around his desk to stand next to Isaac.

Isaac stayed seated and bowed his head, not wanting to tower over the five foot two inch doctor by nearly a foot.

***

Isaac worked late that night to make up for the hours he missed from the job because of the time he spent at the doctor's office, plus the two hour drive to get there. He'd been going to Dr. Carrington in Hempstead, Long Island all his adult life and hadn't taken the time to find a new physician in Mountain Spring in the year that he'd been here.

Who was he kidding? He hadn't worked late to make up for anything. He didn't want to face Elizabeth tonight or ever. He couldn't stand to look in her face and see her smile, the beautiful and deceitful curve of sensational lips that always tilted his heart and mind in crazy ways. All day, he'd thought about what she'd done, the lies she'd told, the pretense, and the charade of caring that she'd kept up since they were married. He'd grown disgusted to the point where he didn't want to see her tonight. Yet, he had to talk to her. He had to let her know that he was onto her. He couldn't pretend ignorance. He wasn't a fraud like she was. Honesty was an important matter to him.

He slowed as he turned onto Meridian Drive and approached the house he'd bought six months ago—the place that had felt like home until tonight with that deceitful woman in it. Mike, his neighbor to the right, was watering his lawn like he usually did at nine o'clock every night. Viola, the woman across the street and who was already on the street when he got here, had taken to reading on her front porch. It looked like she was trying to attract Mike's attention since she straddled the railing and braced her back against an iron pole that had to be uncomfortable. She always had a book open, but Isaac had a feeling it held less of her attention than the man across the street. As for Mike, Isaac wasn't sure if he noticed or not. He did wave and say 'hello' when he came out and saw her, but that was the extent of his neighborly behavior.

Isaac pulled into his driveway and killed the engine. With a one-car garage, he'd deferred to his wife on occupancy since she worked from home and didn't pull out every morning. Reluctant to enter his own house, he wondered if Liz was asleep. The living room light was on which meant negative. He stepped out of the car and headed for his front door and a woman he no longer cared to call his wife.

CHAPTER IX

The morning sickness had passed, and now she craved everything that was bad for her health. She wanted Rugelach, not the vegetarian kind, but the one with the real cheese, cinnamon, and raisins. So far, Elizabeth had eaten six of those today. She'd gained five pounds in the past month, and she didn't think it was all baby weight. She had a mound before her, which showed in her spandex dresses, but with loose fitting blouses, nobody knew she was pregnant.

Isaac had been in disbelief and then ecstatic since she told him she was pregnant last week. He'd been kind of floating all around the house since the announcement of impending fatherhood. Elizabeth looked at her watch: Nine o'clock. He worked late some nights, but he usually called if he wasn't going to be home by six o'clock. There weren't any missed messages to her knowledge.

The sound of the front door unlocking had her turning her head with a welcoming smile. She rose from the sofa and went towards him.

"Hi, I—"

The chill in his countenance froze her words, smile, and her entire body. "What's the matter?" she asked in a rush, her breath catching.

He didn't answer as he sidestepped her and headed to the rear of the house and towards their bedroom.

Confused at his attitude, Elizabeth watched his retreating back. "Isaac?" she called after him uncertainly. A slammed door was his response. Elizabeth's heart moved from missing beats to murdering her rib cage with an almighty pounding. Did he know the truth? Had he found out? On quivering feet, she went to the door and turned the knob.

His back was turned to her. "Isaac, you're making me nervous. What is it? What upset you?"

Tension radiated from his stiff posture and the ramrod straightness of his spine. His briefcase hit the hardwood floor with a thud, loud in the silence, and made Elizabeth jerk.

"*You* upset me, Liz." His words rolled out in a low, rage-filled snarl, and when he turned around, she flinched from the hatred in his face.

She clutched her neck with a shaking hand, forcing words out around the fear in her throat, "Wh-what d-did I do?" *Please, God, please don't let him know the truth.*

"You have the audacity to ask me that," he hissed, approaching her with measured steps and balled hands at his sides.

Elizabeth held her ground only because fleeing would corroborate her guilt. She clutched at a floundering hope that he didn't know the truth.

"I'm going to be a daddy you said, knowing all along that it was a lie!"

"What?" Elizabeth was confused. "I didn't lie. You're going to be a father. I am pregnant."

"Not for me!" he thundered.

Jesus! Oh, Jesus! He knows, but how? Bracing a hand against the nearby dressing table for an anchor as her world tilted towards Hades, she swallowed and tried to talk around the growing aridity in her throat and the fear flooding her heart. She touched her belly, "This baby is yours. You—"

"Stop lying, Elizabeth!" he blasted. "What is wrong with you?! What kind of sick mind do you have that you don't know wrong from right?" His repugnance almost made her wilt with shame. Elizabeth trembled, having no idea what to say. "You *lied* your way into this marriage and tried to lie your way through it. Well, you can stop now because I know this baby *cannot* be mine."

His voice rang with a certainty that was undeniable. Cannot, he'd said. What did he mean? Her heart rattling with terror she asked him.

"I'm infertile, Liz," he admitted through his teeth, the low words making it to audio with evident struggle.

49

Elizabeth sagged against the dressing table. "Oh, God. Oh my, God," she breathed aloud with no awareness of it. The game was over. There was no way she could continue this charade—this lie. *What am I going to do? What will he do?* Trepidation mounting, she dragged her gaze from the floor, fearful of meeting his eyes and too humiliated to do so, but out of options. "I didn't mean to dupe you," she whispered.

"Oh, so you coming onto me all of a sudden like a seductress wasn't all part of the plan to fool me into thinking you cared so I could marry you," he derided.

Elizabeth pressed a hand to her battering heart, trying to still the intensity of its beat. The pace of it made her lightheaded. "In the end, it wasn't," she revealed weakly.

"What was it then?" he demanded.

Elizabeth could not answer that without making the situation worse. "I love you, Isaac," she murmured shakily.

"DON'T!"

She jerked as the shout hit her body like an electrical volt.

"Do *not* lie about that," he snarled. "You have lied about everything in this relationship. Your interest in me was a fabrication, the kisses you gave me forced. Y—"

"Isaa—"

"Shut up and let me finish!" he ordered harshly.

Elizabeth stiffened at the insult. Her heart started knocking from a burgeoning anger now and not solely from fear.

"Your hugs were shared through duty, not desire. Your lovemaking, God, I don't even want to talk about that." He closed his eyes and pressed his fist to his forehead. "All of it was a lie." He opened his eyes and glared at her with escalating contempt. "You endured my touch and doused the light every time so that you wouldn't have to look at a man you didn't love. You close your eyes when I kiss you. Jesus, I don't even know if your orgasms are for real or a lie like every other thing about you."

Elizabeth could hardly breathe. Which part of it could she deny when most of it was the truth? They said truth was stranger than fiction, and while it was easier for her to make love to him if she didn't have to look at his face, during the whole thing, she did love him. Love, she had come to realize, involved more than an appreciation of the outward appearance. She liked his consideration and gentleness, although he was anything but that now. Some men would have expected domestic perfection from a wife who worked at home. He was the type of man who, if he came home to no dinner, he would prepare something and not only for himself. Through some of the women's ministries' meetings at church, she'd heard of women with husbands who expected them to fix three meals, do laundry, keep the house clean, and raise the kids while they worked outside the home. Plus, they wanted sex anytime they felt like it and didn't care if their wives were exhausted. If she told him no, Isaac left her alone. In intimacy, he'd taken time to discover what pleased her instead of focusing only on his needs.

How could she tell him all that was in her head without creating a deeper divide between them and without making him despise her more? She couldn't say in one breath that she loved him, and reveal in the next that she didn't find him attractive physically.

"You can't say anything because you know I'm telling the truth," he accused bitterly. He laughed, a hoarse sound full of rancor. "You won't have to turn out lights, close your eyes, or fake climaxes anymore, because knowing what you've done killed any feelings I had for you. I have no desire to be with you like that anymore, and especially not when you have another man's baby inside of you."

He turned his back and shrugged out of his jacket. "Please leave, I need to change, and I've got to pack some things."

Her heart dropped to the basement and kept searching for an end. Was he leaving her? "Isaac, I know what I've done is despicable, dirty, wicked, and dishonest, but I'm begging you, let's try to work this out," she pleaded. "I know you don't believe it, but I do love you. Don't divorce me, please, and don't leave me."

He spun around and gave her an incredulous stare. "Leave you? This is *my* house. I'm not walking away from it. I'm simply moving out of this room. If you want to go, feel free," he declared callously, flinging his arm towards the door and sending a piercing hurt knifing through her heart. "And if you want to divorce me, go ahead." He stopped and tilted his head one side as if considering that. "But you won't do that because you need to be respectably married to cover up your fornication with whomever that pregnancy belongs to."

He turned away again and threw some final words over his

shoulder. "And don't waste your breath telling me you love me. I don't believe you and never will, again. Now, please leave."

"Isaac I—" she tried again.

"GET OUT!!!" he bellowed.

Elizabeth fled the room on trembling legs.

CHAPTER X

Elizabeth stared at the time on the alarm clock on her nightstand: 11:00 p.m. The red numbers shone piercingly in an otherwise darkened room, reminding her of spilled blood. She felt like blood had been let in the earlier verbal battle between her and her husband. She watched the digits on the clock change for the next five minutes, searching in vain for sleep. She had papers to correct, but couldn't find the focus to do them. Her mind was full of the argument that she'd had with Isaac and the painful things he'd said to her. She'd tried to talk to him when he came out of their room but he'd barked at her and ordered her to stay away from him. Liz still tried to apologize, but he simply ignored her the entire time. After a while she kept silent, understanding that every word she spoke met a wall of resistance, bounced off, and fell into a pile of failure since Isaac had resolved to tune her out.

A month ago when she married him, she had entered the union out of expedience and not from any desire to be married and especially not to him. In a short time, he'd grown on her with his gentleness and thoughtfulness. He knew her online class schedule and showed up about three times during her break between classes to take her to lunch. Other times, he'd just brought her food when he couldn't adjust his lunch hour to hers. She liked to read; he discovered her favorite authors and bought her books. True to his word, he did the laundry most of the time and ironed her clothes as well as his.

Initially, she automatically returned his morning wake-up and farewell kisses before he went to work without any genuine feelings.

She said 'I love you,' because he always did it first and she felt obligated to reciprocate it. In the last two weeks, however, the feelings in her heart towards her husband had started moving beyond pleasant tolerance to genuine affection. She looked forward to his phone calls, and his lunch hour visits. At night, she still turned out the light but loved him back with freedom now rather than faking it.

Elizabeth hugged the extra pillow on the bed and wished it were Isaac. How could she open up the lines of communication between them? Her voice made him angry, as did her presence. Should she try to get them into counseling so that they could work this problem out? Did he even want to? From what he'd said to her earlier, he didn't. Elizabeth knew that she had to impress upon him the genuineness of her regret for what she had done. But how would she do that if he didn't want to listen to her? *Make him.* Elizabeth blinked at the clear voice in her head. Make him how? Her thoughts chased each other, trying to answer the question, and then like adhesive peeling off the back of a label, understanding flooded her mind. Elizabeth threw back the covers, knowing exactly what she needed to do.

***

Isaac roused groggily from the recent sleep that had claimed his despondent body. Something warm and soft pressed against his back while a private place pulsed from the stimulation of a soft and skillful touch. *What?* He opened his eyes and stared in confusion into the dark. When a leg thrust over his and a warm kiss touched his nape, fury shot through him like a firecracker. He threw himself from the bed and flipped the lamp on.

He glared at Elizabeth, lying there with not one stitch of clothing and staring at him as if his reaction wasn't the outcome she had expected.

"What do you think you're doing?" he demanded.

"Trying to apologize," she whispered.

"Like this?" he asked incredulously.

"I didn't know any other way," she said softly.

"I'm sorry would have been a start," he said, watching her with a disgusted gaze.

She bit her lip at his sarcastic tone and her eyes fell from the anger in his. "I tried that earlier and you tuned me out," she reminded him in a small voice.

"And you thought *this* was better?" He looked at her as if he thought she'd lost her mind.

"I didn't know what else to do!" she cried, pushing to her knees.

He gritted his teeth against his rising reaction to her shifting and unbound bosom.

"I'm so sorry, Isaac, for my untruthfulness, but I was desperate. I didn't know what else to do. I'm asking you to forgive me, please."

He ran a hand over his head and sighed. "Elizabeth, I don't want to talk about this right now. Please get out of my room and don't come back in here like this again." He flicked a disparaging finger at her state of undress. "And get this into your head: You cannot use your body to buy my forgiveness. When I'm ready, if ever I'm ready, I'll do it because I want to and not because you coerced me into it."

"Isaac, I'm not trying to coerce you into anything," she objected, getting off the bed and moving towards him.

"Put some clothes on, Elizabeth!" he ordered sharply.

She wrapped the sheet around her, filing away his reaction. His tension revealed that he wasn't immune to her—he just wished to be because of what she had done. "I'm trying to convince you that I regret what I did," she continued.

"Don't start with that," he said in annoyance, tossing her words aside with an impatient hand. "You didn't regret a thing until I found out. If I hadn't caught you in the lie, you would have had no regrets."

"That's not true. I hated that I wasn't forthright with you from the beginning, Isaac. I'm being sincere about that." She took a small step towards him and held his angry gaze with a pleading one of her own. "Please try to look at things from my perspective. I was a single, Christian woman who was pregnant for a married man."

Elizabeth stopped and bit her lip at his shocked expression. She hadn't meant to confess that part, but it was just as well because she needed to come totally clean if she hoped to move forward in this marriage on a new page. "I know that I'm the worst kind of sinner, but it wasn't something I planned," she told him, as if that could make it any less repulsive, and that was how he was watching her now—as if she were regurgitated material rather than his wife.

"Sin is sin. No matter the act, it is wrong and awful." His remark was not an effort at comfort. The coldness and scorn in his statement made that clear. "I just hope to God that you are done with this married lover of yours and that he is nowhere near here."

Guilt gave her away and made Elizabeth's eyes slide away from her husband's at that remark. It was very close to home.

Isaac shook his head. "He's here in Mountain Spring, isn't he?" he demanded, glaring at her.

Elizabeth swallowed. "Does it matter? It's over between us. He has no bearing on our lives now."

He laughed in disbelief. "No bearing?" he repeated, staring pointedly at her stomach. "Honey, I think he has a great deal of bearing on our lives. You're carrying his child."

"Which he doesn't know about."

"Right," Isaac snorted in derision. "He doesn't need to because you've got a ready made father for his kid—me." He stepped closer and got in her face. "Let me make something clear to you, Liz, you got a husband out of this trick you pulled, but you will *not* get a father for that baby out of it! I'm not taking on another man's burden."

Elizabeth could take any abuse from him for herself. She'd harmed him, but this child she carried was innocent of adults' foolishness, and she would not allow her husband to disparage him or her. Placing a protective hand over the mound of her belly, she declared with breathless vehemence, "My baby is *not* a burden, and I won't allow you to reference this precious soul as such. If you were thinking with more than injured feelings, you'd realize that this could be your gift from God since you can't father a kid for yourself!"

Elizabeth dropped the sheet and stalked out of the room, slamming the door behind her. Maybe she should have tried single-motherhood instead of this grand plan of respectable married woman. It wasn't working out so well at all.

CHAPTER XI

Elizabeth stared out onto New Street, watching the traffic and pedestrians congest the road and sidewalk during the lunch hour in downtown Mountain Spring. The voices of her sisters filtered around her. They were at their weekly meeting at Connie's Café, but Elizabeth hadn't wanted to come today. With unhappiness in her home weighing her down for the past two months, it was getting increasingly difficult to maintain a façade of contentment when she felt depressed. After her final remark to her husband about his need to be thankful for the baby since he couldn't impregnate a woman, Isaac had not spoken to her much less looked at her. They passed each other in the house like sworn enemies, neither of the two talking. The tension in their home was thicker than the concrete outside the Café on New Street's sidewalk. Its weight was heavier than the eighteen-wheeler in the municipal parking across the street.

"Elizabeth, what's wrong with you?"

She dragged herself out of her disconsolate thoughts and focused on Karen who had asked the question. "Nothing. Why do you think something is wrong?" she asked, forcing a smile.

"Because you're not paying attention, haven't been for a while."

"A while as in the past three times we met," Dri added her two cents. "What's the matter? Is everything okay at home?"

Elizabeth knew her sister asked out of concern, but maybe didn't expect the answer that she gave. What came out of her mouth simply flew out because she was full, tired of pretending, and it just overflowed. "No, everything's not okay," she murmured, dropping her face in her hands.

A hush fell over the table as seconds sped away. Adrianna broke it and spoke first. She shifted her chair closer to Liz's left and slipped an arm around her sister. Karen did the same on the other side.

"It's okay, baby," Dri soothed her as she began to cry.

"I'm not a baby. I'm a woman about to have a baby," she blubbered. Both her sisters referred to her as baby since she was the last girl. Emotionally overwrought now, the reference bothered her since she was anything but that. Rather, she was a woman alone, facing the huge responsibility of raising a child by herself and providing all of its needs without help from her husband, since he wasn't the father and refused to be.

"I know, honey," Dri murmured. "I'm just trying to comfort you."

"I don't know what do," Elizabeth confessed, taking the napkin Karen offered and wiping her eyes and nose.

"About what?" Karen asked.

"About my baby and about my marriage."

Silence again. "I think you need to expand on that, Liz," Dri said, "because I'm lost and Karen looks like she is, too."

Liz glanced at Karen to see her brow furrowed. She found Adrianna's the same way when she looked. "Isaac's not the father of this baby," she announced.

Her sisters' mouths opened and closed, each fighting for something to say, but obviously not finding any words.

"Who's the father?" Karen blurted.

"Karen," Dri chided, "Maybe she can't say."

Elizabeth was full and wanted to confess everything. "It's Terence."

More silence.

"You mean the one from church?" Dri asked, sounding like she hoped for a negative answer.

Elizabeth nodded.

"Lord have mercy," Karen breathed. "He's married, Liz." The statement, though horrified, didn't condemn.

"What happened? I mean, how did you get involved in a mess like that?" Karen asked, again without censure but more with disbelief.

Elizabeth covered her face again. "It was one night of poor judgment."

Adrianna sighed as if she understood, which she did because she'd slept with a married man, although, she'd been unaware of his status at the time. "I had one of those." She admitted aloud something her sisters already knew.

"Well, even though a baby came out of it, thank God it wasn't a full blown affair like Dri's situation," Karen said, trying to find dawn in the darkness. "No offence, Dri," she tagged on with a quick smile at the older girl.

Adrianna shrugged. "None taken. I'm glad it was a one-time thing. The other type can destroy your soul and salvation."

They noticed Elizabeth wasn't saying anything.

"It was a one time thing, wasn't it?" Karen asked her.

She shook her head.

"Oh, God," Adrianna said, lifting her eyes to the ceiling. "Liz, how long did this go on..." she trailed off, and tagged on in a hushed voice, "It's done, right? I mean you *are* married."

Karen straightened in her seat as Elizabeth slowly lifted her head to take in the alarmed gazes of her sisters. "Liz?" she prompted.

"I'm not seeing him now. He ended it almost four months ago."

From the shifting expressions of wonder, bafflement, and incredulity on Dri's and Karen's faces, Elizabeth could tell that about a million questions were racing around in their brains, probably rushing too fast for them to make sense of their thoughts.

"How long did the affair last?" Karen asked.

"Two years."

"Is that why you moved to Mountain Spring? To be with him?" Adrianna's eyes were very wide with amazement.

Elizabeth shook her head. "I met him within a month of coming here."

"Where?"

"Remember, that Labor Day church picnic in Washington Park?"

Dri nodded.

"I met him there and things escalated. He was lonely and things weren't working out at home. Foolish me, I was attracted to him and let it grow, although I shouldn't have entertained it or him since he belonged to somebody else. After that first time, it's like I couldn't stop and got deeper and deeper." Elizabeth stopped speaking, hearing her voice and offended by her words. When she thought back on it, she'd been weak and without fortitude or conscience. *Lord, I need so much purging, so much washing.*

"The blessing is that you stopped the foolishness."

"Two years late," Elizabeth said bitterly.

"Better late than never," Karen said.

Elizabeth appreciated their support and encouragement. She decided not to confess her sin with Terence after the breakup. Some things were best mentioned to God alone. He was the one person you could share anything with, no matter how despicable, and He would still keep you close while humans would shun you.

"How much older is the pregnancy than your marriage?" Adrianna asked, her eyes falling towards the direction of Elizabeth's belly, which the table hid.

"Nearly two months," she confessed.

"That means you're in the second trimester."

She nodded. "I'm twenty weeks."

"You said earlier that you didn't know what to do about your marriage," Karen put in. "Does Isaac know the baby's not his?"

"I told him." She paused. "Well, he found out."

"That's the worse way to get information—by accident." Karen spoke as if from experience. "I suppose he was angry."

"That's mild," Elizabeth murmured, remembering his rage.

"Livid?" Adrianna supplied.

"Close. I've never seen him like that. He screamed at me, told me to shut up, and said he didn't want any part of a body that had betrayed him and carried another man's seed."

"Lord, he told you all that?" Karen grimaced.

"Not in so many words, but pretty much."

"Clear up something for me," Adrianna said, a frown ruffling her eyebrows. "You said he found out the baby wasn't his. How?"

"He's infertile."

"Say what?!" Karen exclaimed while Adrianna's groomed brows raised the bar on sky-high.

"Did you know?" Adrianna asked, back to frowning even heavier than before.

Elizabeth shook her head. "I'm not sure that he knew."

"What do you mean?" Dri asked.

"He went to the doctor on the day he told me that he was. I assumed he found out that day."

"You assumed?" Adrianna gave her a skeptical look. "You didn't ask?"

"At the time, I was more focused on the fact that he'd found me out and the possibility I might be facing divorce. I didn't think to examine the details behind his infertile claim."

"Liz, an infertility check is not something that's a part of a routine doctors' visit or not something doctors check for in a physical," Adrianna explained. " A man's fertility comes into question when the woman he's with cannot get pregnant. You were already pregnant, why then would he get his fertility checked?"

Elizabeth borrowed Adrianna's frown in a superlative degree. Beleaguered with the distance and discord between her and her husband, she hadn't thought about all Dri had just said, but her sister made a lot of sense. "I don't know," she answered Adrianna's question. "Unless he was already infertile and hid it from me."

Adrianna gave her a there-you-go-look and sat back in her seat.

Elizabeth considered the possibility she just articulated. Although her heart caught a little with indignation that she wasn't the only one not forthright in the matter of truth, she didn't get angry. Rather, she experienced a little relief that her husband wasn't a paragon of virtue. Maybe it would help her case when she next pleaded with him for forgiveness. What did the scriptures say? "He that is without sin among you, let him first cast a stone at her" (John 8:7).

"Although it looks like both of you hid things from each other," Karen began, giving Elizabeth an earnest look, "the question is, do you want to move forward? Do you want to try to fix things?"

Elizabeth met her searching gaze and answered as honestly as she could, "I can only speak for myself, Karen. I want to fix this, but I don't know what Isaac wants."

"Have you asked him?"

"I haven't got any encouragement to do that."

"If it's encouragement you're looking for, don't expect any, at least not right now. Men don't forgive quickly when you dupe them the way you did your husband. I think Karen will agree with me on this."

Karen nodded.

"You know what we did with our respective husbands and the hell we went through with them."

Elizabeth remembered how Adrianna had gotten pregnant without telling her husband, Christopher, making him believe she was taking birth control when she wasn't. Their marriage almost fell apart when he learned of her duplicity, for he never wanted children after how his first wife and baby died. Karen, on the other hand, had married her husband and left him as payback for an old injury. God, however, overturned her plan, and she got pregnant, lost her job and had to return to a man who now hated her. They made it, as well, but only after a great deal of heartache and unhappiness. Both her sisters acknowledged that they were married today solely because of God's grace and mercy.

"You have to do all the reaching out," Adrianna said. "And you'll hit a brick wall half the time."

"Sounds familiar," Elizabeth muttered.

"Because he's still mad, his pride is injured, and he's hurt. But if you love him, you shake off his smart and hurtful remarks, breathe hard, and keep trying, all the while praying like crazy."

"Do you love him, Liz?" Karen asked.

"I do now," she admitted.

Karen smiled. "That's all you need, baby sister. Love can endure and conquer all things. I know. I've lived it."

"I've been struggling with the praying part, though. I've done so many bad things. I ignored the Holy Spirit speaking to me and basically disowned God and His ways. I feel like a fraud going to Him now that I need help when I didn't listen before."

"God sacrificed His son for sinners, Liz, not for the righteous. So there's nothing that you can do to make God hate you. If you realize your wrong, tell it to Him, and ask for pardon. He'll forgive you in less than a heart murmur," Karen encouraged her.

Bible texts that their father, Pastor Alfred Monroe, taught them about God's great mercy and love came to Liz. She remembered texts she hadn't recited in years since her father died and since she went contrary to her Christian beliefs. Scriptures like "For I have satiated the weary soul, and I have replenished every sorrowful soul" (Jeremiah 31:25) and "...If any man thirst, let him come unto me and drink" (John 7:37).

"Thanks, Karen, I'll do that," she said. Reaching out, she squeezed her sister's hand and gave her a grateful smile. "And thanks, Dri, for the advice; and to both of you, thanks for listening."

They did a three-way hug.

"I think we should pray," Adrianna suggested. "Karen, since you're the pastor's wife," she teased, "you pray."

Karen made a face at her. "Okay," she agreed. "Before I do, though, I have one more question for you, Liz." She turned to her sister. "Does Isaac know who the baby's father is?"

"No, I didn't tell him," Elizabeth shook her head.

"My advice: keep it to yourself. Let it remain secret."

"I agree," Adrianna spoke up in support. "Right now, concentrate on healing the rift between both of you. Let's pray."

CHAPTER XII

McBride's Gym the next morning.

"Man, are you okay?" Terence asked, casting a wary glance towards Isaac who seemed to be battling demons with the heavy bag in the boxing room.

Isaac drove two powerful jabs and a right cross before responding. Breathing hard, he wiped sweat from his brow with the back of his hand and answered Terence abruptly. "No, I'm not."

"Do you want to talk about it?" Terence offered an ear.

Isaac mulled over the invitation, and then reluctantly admitted, "The problem is a little personal."

Terence smiled in understanding, turning to his own heavy bag. "Usually," he started, "when a man has that kind of issue," he punched his bag, three rapid and successive hits, "it's either a woman or his privates."

Isaac's heart jerked at the accuracy of his statement. Should he share his problems with Terence? He desperately wanted to tell somebody. He thought about Pastor Watson, but he was his brother-in-law. Would the man be objective about the problem between him and Liz when he was a relative? Besides, he didn't know what Liz had already told her sisters. Suppose her sister Karen, Pastor Watson's wife, shared what Liz told her with her husband. The pastor's objectivity would be compromised, wouldn't it? Even though he was selective about whom he told, Isaac felt like it was choking him and eating him up inside at the way Liz had deceived him. Not only did he feel inadequate

64

from being unable to impregnate her, he felt even less of a man that his wife married him on the rebound and as a last resort. He was not a natural choice for her, but an unavoidable selection, something that under normal circumstances she would never have done. "What if I said that it's both?" he asked Terence quietly.

Terence stopped punching at once and held the heavy bag steady. "I'd say you have a serious problem. I'll listen if you want to talk."

"It's not something that's easy to share with anyone and especially not a guy."

Terence shrugged. "No pressure if you don't want to." He turned back and delivered one close range upper cut to the bag.

"What would you do if your wife was pregnant for another man?"

He watched Terence stiffen, and turn to him. "What are you saying?"

Isaac heard the guardedness in his tone but was so deeply embroiled in the frustration, hurt, and embarrassment of his problem that he didn't pay much attention. "I already said it, man." Isaac let the hypothetical question stand since it pretty much told the truth.

"I'm not saying you should do this, but I couldn't stay with a woman who cheated on me like that."

"She didn't cheat."

Terence frowned. "What do you mean? She's pregnant for another man while she's married to you. That's only possible by cheating."

"She was pregnant before I married her."

"Sh—" He slapped a hand over his mouth to stifle the curse. "Man," Terence looked around and sidled closer so the guys nearby wouldn't hear. "You sure?"

"Of course I'm sure," Isaac almost snapped, irritated.

"So you mean nothing's been happening?" Terence asked, his voice lower than before. *She must miss me if she's not giving him any action.*

Isaac frowned, not following him for a moment, and then he got it. "Well, nothing's happened since I found out what she did, but before it was all good."

Terence frowned now. "So how do you know it's not your kid she's having?"

Isaac shifted in sudden discomfort, beginning to regret his decision to confide in Terence. The guy was a member of his church, and while they were gym buddies, it never boded well to let church people know your business. But he thought about how the man had shared his own personal problems with him some weeks ago. Isaac didn't think Terence would be the type to let his business out, especially since he knew stuff about the guy. "Look, this part is really difficult." He paused, took a breath, and huffed it out. "I can't have kids," he muttered.

"Huh?"

"I'm infertile," Isaac gritted.

Terence stared hard at him, swept the room again, and shifted into his personal space. "Low sperm count, you mean?" he whispered.

Isaac glanced about uneasily, knowing that others couldn't have heard, but still checking. This wasn't something you wanted anybody to know about you. "Yeah, that's what I mean."

"Man, I'm sorry," Terence said, appearing truly distressed for him. "That's hard."

"Yeah, it's something I have to live with."

"Does your wife know?"

"I told her when I confronted her about the pregnancy and she tried to insist that it was mine."

"I supposed that killed her whole argument," Terence observed.

"Pretty much."

"What are you going to do? Stay in the marriage?"

"I'm really not sure what to do, Terence. I don't believe in divorce, but I don't see how I can live forever in the current circumstance."

"What circumstance is that?"

"The environment is so tense at home that I'm more tired being there than from going to work. Liz and I aren't talking. We pass each other like the other one is invisible. If we end up in the same room together, we're shifting around like two idiots, trying not to bump into one another. It's well past uncomfortable now. I can't live like that forever." Isaac heaved a huge sigh, glad he got his inner thoughts off his chest on the one hand, but feeling burdened anew that he hadn't found a solution for his situation.

"You're right," Terence agreed. "You can't live like that. I know it's hard. I can imagine you're upset with her right now to the point where you can't stand to see her. It was that way with me and Sonja. That's how I stepped out."

"I don't plan to step out," Isaac said sharply.

Terence's smile was wry. "It's not something you plan, man. It just happens."

"Well, I'm not putting myself into that situation."

"You already did. With the trouble, I take it that you're not sleeping with your wife. Right?"

"No, I'm not and don't want to."

Excellent. Excellent. "Well, you've got a man's needs. If you don't ease it with your wife, and if you stay that way long enough, you'll ease it with somebody else."

He said it with such confidence that Isaac gave him a troubled look, wondering if he had a point.

"The other thing you might want to realize, and I'm talking to you as a friend who's had some rough marital times, is that women can start feeling neglected also and aren't averse to stepping out." *Seed of doubt planted.*

Isaac shot him a sharp look. "You think Liz will step out on me since we're not sleeping together?"

Terence lifted clueless shoulders. "I don't know her, so I don't know how she thinks." *I know her very well and she likes action and often.* "But I'm just saying, whatever you're doing, do quickly. If it's separation, then do it. If you're going to try to fix things, then do it." *Please don't. Follow the first one.*

Isaac looked at his watch. It was almost time to leave. "Thanks, Terence, for listening and for the advice. I really appreciate it," he said, shaking the other man's hand. "I was full and had to talk to somebody."

"No problem. I hope everything works out between you and Liz." *Do not!*

"I hope so." His response was automatic, and Isaac realized the truth was what came from his heart. He hated what his wife did, but his love hadn't died. He was not yet ready to reconcile, though.

"I'll say a prayer for you both," Terence offered. *Will not!*

"Please do. We need it. See you tomorrow." Isaac walked away, appreciative of the man's offer, and not realizing what he'd just done was to give the devil ammunition against him and his marriage.

CHAPTER XIII

That evening, Elizabeth took her sisters' advice to heart. Once again, she decided to reach out to her husband, knowing she was risking another snub, but refusing to give up on a marriage that had become real to her. In their short union, she'd learned what foods he liked. He was partial to split peas soup and liked sweet potatoes in it—an oddity to her way of thinking, but she made it to please him. She'd bought some Italian bread from the store to go with that and had converted some of it into garlic bread. As the heat rose in the oven, garlic, herbs, spices, and Italian seasoning meshed and perfumed the air with a mouth-watering scent. Elizabeth labored over her mother's seasoned rice recipe, trying to remember all the ingredients to get the unique and satisfying flavor that accompanied that recipe. She called her to see if she forgot anything, but Mrs. Monroe wasn't home. Karen didn't pick up either, and Elizabeth didn't waste time calling Dri because she hated cooking and never learned the art too well. Her effort paid off when the cooking was done. She helped herself to enough of it that she might not be able to actually get any food in at dinnertime.

Elizabeth checked the stir-fried Brussels sprouts and string beans, making sure they didn't overcook on the low flame. She looked at the kitchen's clock: Eight o'clock. Any minute Isaac should be home. Elizabeth rushed into the bathroom and checked her appearance. Her freshly washed and styled hair, fell to her shoulders. The huge curls, combed out now, gave fullness to the style, which flipped up at the ends courtesy of a curling iron. Her face was scrubbed clean, and there was a glow to it that Karen and Dri attributed to the pregnancy. Since they were the experts, she yielded to their opinion and thought that maybe she'd spend less on skin care products, if pregnancy enhanced her skin this much. She wore a white caftan with a wide boat neckline, and wondered briefly if she should change it with the swells of her breasts flashing at the neckline. She shrugged the thought away. This was her home, and she was dining in with her husband, a man she was trying to reconcile with. A little bit of skin in sight could only help, even though he hadn't minced words when he said she couldn't buy his forgiveness with her body.

Elizabeth heard the key turning in the lock and hurried to the door. She opened it before he could push it inwards. The smile she sent him was brilliant. The look he leveled at her was unguarded. She saw everything that she could hope for that the evening would go well: need, sexual hunger, regret, and mixed in with that were embers of love. He quickly hid his emotions from her.

She smiled at him. "Hi, Isaac."

"Hi," he said shortly and started to step around her.

Elizabeth reached for his briefcase, slid her fingers through the handle, and tugged. "Let me take this from you."

He held fast. "No thanks." His objection was more abrupt than his greeting.

"I made dinner," she offered, trying to distract him from the death grip he had on the case.

"That's nice, but I'm not hungry." He moved off down the hall.

Elizabeth walked with him to prevent him dragging her along since she hadn't released his briefcase. She ignored the dip her heart took at his dismissive tone and disinterest in all the effort she'd made to prepare dinner. Be persistent and roll with the punches. Dri and Karen had said something to that effect. "I've got split peas soup with sweet potatoes," she offered with an encouraging smile.

He stopped at his bedroom door, and searched her face while his expression shifted from irritated to suspicious. "What do you want, Liz?"

To fix our marriage. "To have dinner with you," she said hopefully.

"There's no 'with you' where we're concerned anymore."

Elizabeth felt her patience sprinting away. She took a mental breath. "Isaac, its just dinner. You make it sound like I have some kind of conspiracy planned."

"And you don't think I'm justified with the foolishness you've already pulled?"

Elizabeth had no rebuttal to his sarcastic words. What could she say? She was guilty. It was undeniable. "You're right," she said quietly. "You're right to be suspicious of me. I've been dishonest. You don't trust me. I understand, but I'm trying to earn your trust, and I've told you the truth. I came clean. I'd like to have dinner with you and I'd like to talk to you. I'm being honest about that. Will you have dinner with me, Isaac?"

The Barber family at the end of the street must have heard his sigh. Elizabeth bit her lip and crossed her fingers. He released the briefcase to her, propped one hand on a lean hip, and scrubbed the other down his face. Resistance to her request was present in the stiff lines of his body and the reluctance in his face.

"Please," she tagged on, hoping to sway him towards an affirmative.

"Let me wash my hands. I'll be there." He walked away after the abrupt agreement.

Elizabeth had all the food on the table by the time he joined her. She flicked a quick glance at him as she placed serving spoons in the various dishes. He'd changed, at least partially—he still wore his dress shirt. His tie was gone, his shirtsleeves folded back, and he'd switched his suit pants for a pair of cargos. "Sit down, everything's ready," she invited, smiling at him.

He sat without returning her smile. Elizabeth worked to stop the wobble in hers. She didn't expect this to be easy; but it didn't seem like Isaac planned to help smooth the way at all.

"Will you pray?" she asked, taking her seat and closing her eyes. When she heard nothing after several seconds, she peeked. Isaac stared at her as if he didn't understand her and didn't like her.

When their eyes met, he said, "You pray, Liz. I can't."

Elizabeth's heart thumped. That didn't sound favorable. "Why can't you pray?" She didn't know what else to say.

"How can you ask me that?" he demanded with a scowl.

Elizabeth lifted her shoulders, not understanding why he was getting angry over a simple prayer. "All you have to do is thank God for the meal," she murmured.

"I can't do that, Liz, not when I'm angry with you about the mess you made of this marriage," he accused. "I can't sit here and pretend that this," he gestured at the food on the table, "is a normal everyday meal between a couple because it's not. There's nothing normal about our relationship anymore. I cannot be a hypocrite and sit here making trite conversation with you when there's no peace between us. I—"

"I want—"

He held up a hand. "Please let me finish."

Elizabeth closed her mouth and followed the pattern on the damask tablecloth as he kept talking.

"I cannot pray when my heart is full of the hurt you caused me and when my spirit is heavy with your dishonesty. I can't do it when I know all this effort you expended is to try to fix things to save this institution of marriage you entered to stop the shame of your having sex before marriage. And I can't do this when I know you have no true desire to reconcile with me personally."

He pushed his chair back and rose from the table. Elizabeth hurried to his side, her head empty of ideas, save for an urgent prayer for the Lord to give her words of wisdom to speak to her husband. She caught his arm in both her hands, stopping his exit. "Don't go," she pleaded. "What you said isn't true and isn't right. I'm not trying to save the marriage, I'm trying to win you, Isaac."

"Liz, I'm tired, and I had to bring work home, so I have a long night ahead. I don't have time to waste listening to more of your lies." His voice was weary as were his dark brown eyes, now watching her without emotion. "This whole relationship was never about me and my needs. It was about you in the brief time we dated, and it's still about you." He tried to step around her, but Elizabeth didn't let him.

Her heart pounding, she tried again to break through the barrier he'd created between them. "I know that I've been inconsiderate and selfish, but I want to change that and I am trying, Isaac, but I need you to at least consider working things out between us. It's not going to work if I'm the only one making an effort to save our relationship."

He gazed at her as if she were slow. "There is no relationship, Liz. There never was," he said flatly, his disengaged tone confirming a deep belief in what he'd just said. Elizabeth's heart plummeted. If he had no

71

hope in a future, then she was fighting a losing battle. There had to be at least a glimmer of optimism that they could work things out in his mind; if not, then all of her attempts to win him back would be futile.

"How can you say that?" she asked, words coming out of her mouth without direction or any thought of merging them into coherence. Elizabeth was scrambling for something to combat his pessimism and was coming up empty. "I am your wife in every sense of the word. As far as I know, we had a relationship, a good one up until our disagreement."

"Disagreement?" he spat, dragging his arm away. "A disagreement is a mild difference of opinion. What we have is a massive, jagged, irreparable tear in this so-called marital union."

"Please don't say that," she whispered, placing a trembling hand over her mouth and wrapping an arm around her abdomen at the sudden ache she felt there. "Please don't say 'irreparable' because we can fix this, if we both are willing."

"I'm not sure we can do that," he doubted. "I don't know when you're telling the truth. If I can't believe what you say and do, how can we build a relationship? If I doubt your honesty, how can I trust you and the love that you claim you have?"

"Don't you think we have something to fight for?" she asked, searching for some ray of hope in his detached gaze. "I do, Isaac. You keep dismissing it when I say it, but I love you and hope that you love me still."

When his wooden stare remained unchanged, her already shaky confidence faltered, and she asked a question that pride fought to choke. "Do you still love me, Isaac?"

He kept quiet for so long that Elizabeth started believing the reply could only be negative.

"I gave you my heart, and you toyed with it and then ripped it apart."

She flinched, the effect of the final verb painful.

"I may be slow to catch on to a beautiful user like you, but I'm not a fool, Elizabeth. I'm not opening up myself to anymore heartache from you. I will not give you more emotional ammunition to use against me, so I will *never* again speak words to you that will give you power over my emotions."

He tried to sidestep her again, but Elizabeth blocked him, feeling the weight of his pain, and hurting that she'd caused it. "I n-never meant t-to do t-that," she stuttered. She grasped the hands that hung limply at his sides and wrapped her hands around the fists he made. "I'm sorry that I hurt you. I'm sorry that I lied. This is no excuse, but I was desperate and didn't think you'd accept me if I told you I was carrying somebody else's child." She paused and watched his reaction to that. His eyes slid away from hers. "You wouldn't have, would you?"

"I don't know."

Elizabeth swallowed and accepted his honesty. She pressed on. "The fact that you're uncertain now, I hope you can better understand why I was fearful of telling you." She squeezed his hands. "Isaac, I'm sorry that this baby isn't biologically yours and I wish I could perform a miracle that could change that, but I can't. All I can do is ask forgiveness from you and beg you to give this marriage, me, a chance to love you like you deserve, to love you like I'm capable of. All I'm asking is that you give us a chance to turn a new page, and I promise you, that I'll never again give you cause to doubt the truth of my words or my action. Please, Isaac, please give us a chance?"

Elizabeth bowed her head, out of words, bereft of entreaties, empty of emotions. She felt drained, wrung out, and as if she had given her all, her best shot and was unsure if it met the mark, what with her husband's continued silence.

Hurt battled forgiveness and doubt fought belief. *Is her request for reconciliation genuine? Can I believe anything she says ever again without second-guessing it and her motive?* Isaac scoured Elizabeth's face, trying to find anything to contradict the earnestness written across her features. Her eyes pleaded for understanding, shimmering with tears starting to overflow. Her mouth trembled in distress, which seemed too real to be an act. Her hands squeezed his in tight entreaty. Isaac didn't want to continue living in the present tense-filled and unhappy circumstances; but he'd been hoodwinked, taken advantage of, and burned. It was a terrible feeling to learn that he'd been a means to an end. So the difficulty he now had believing her apology and about-face was huge. Did she deserve a chance? *Do you deserve one?* Isaac blinked at the echo in his head. He didn't need chances. He didn't do anything. *Didn't you?* The answer came before the echo died down. He had also withheld something critical in this relationship. Infertility was crucial, and Elizabeth had deserved the right to know that he might never give her children. Yet, fear that she would reject him stopped him sharing that very private problem. The knowledge he withheld was serious. In that moment, he realized the weight of what they'd both failed to tell each other was equal. Right then, Isaac realized that he, like his wife, needed a second chance.

After a long time, he tipped her chin up. With gentle fingers, he brushed her tears away and cupped her cheek. "Look at me, Liz," he commanded soberly.

Elizabeth lifted her lashes and met his serious gaze.

"I'm not a handsome man," he began. "I know that. My ears are prominent, my nose too big, my lips too thick, my body not the most muscular, and to top it off, I can't give you kids." He stopped and Elizabeth's heart caught as his Adam's apple slid up and down, evidence of the impact of his last statement. She rested her hand on his, pressing it against her cheek to show her empathy that way. "I'm sorry I didn't tell you that. It was wrong. Chalk it up to fear of losing the best thing that ever happened to me relationship-wise. You knew all of that, with the exception of the last, before you married me." He leaned close and kissed her cheek.

Elizabeth trembled, feeling a wind of hope blowing in the room, giving rising encouragement that God was fixing their future.

"There's one more thing I didn't tell you."

She looked at him curiously. "What?"

"Six years ago, I left church and got involved in a relationship."

This was news. She'd never have believed him the type to be promiscuous. Well, she never believed she'd been the type either, until it happened to her.

"She traveled a lot. She was a flight attendant. Long story short, she wanted kids but not marriage. I wanted both, so we parted ways. I came back to church; she never did. Shortly after we broke up, she did get pregnant. She called and was happy to tell me that her new guy did what I couldn't."

"Isaac, I'm so sorry," Elizabeth said, feeling for him.

He smiled and shrugged, but deep down, she knew it must hurt, especially with his infertility problem.

"She told me she hadn't been taking birth control in our last months together, and since she was now pregnant, the problem was with me. A man takes that kind of accusation seriously. I did, got checked, and found out she was right. That's how I knew I had a low sperm count."

Elizabeth kissed him. "Her loss is my gain."

He ran his thumb over her cheek in response. "I don't believe in divorce," he said, "but if you want one, I'll give it to you because I should have told you about my infertility."

She shook her head vehemently. "I don't want a divorce. I want you."

He wrapped his arms around her and buried his face in her hair. "God, Liz, I hope you mean that."

"I do," she reiterated, hugging him as tightly as she could without squeezing her belly.

"I need to get one final thing clear, Elizabeth, and I want you to look me dead in the eye as I say it."

They eased away from each other, and their eyes met and held.

"If in the course of this reconciliation," Isaac started, "you decide that you want to be intimate with me, be prepared to make love in the light. I don't want you to endure my touch, Elizabeth; I want you to enjoy it. If you can't do that, then we can stay married without the mating part."

Elizabeth studied her husband's face and wondered what about it had repelled her before. Yes, you noticed his ears before anything else about him. Come to think about it, it was kind of cute. His lips were chunky, but the only thing she thought about when she viewed them was how great they felt against hers. And, yes, his eyes were on the small side, but so what? He probably wouldn't win a poster pin up guy contest or make the cover of a magazine as best looking man of the year. But he was her man, acquired by underhanded means, yet by God's grace willing to forgive rather than forsake her, and she loved him. Elizabeth wound her arms around Isaac's neck and pressed close to him. "If sex is off the table, then I want a divorce."

Her frankness startled him, and she grinned as his eyebrows nearly flew off his face. She kissed him with all the hunger that had piled up in the weeks since that explosive argument. When she drew back, he came after her mouth and the kiss he laid on her heated up the room and the food that had begun to get cold.

"So you know," Elizabeth panted when he gave her a bit of time to breathe, "I don't *endure* your touch. I enjoy your fingers finding my sweet and secret spots so much that I'm excited just thinking about having your hands on my body."

Silence reigned a while after that declaration.

"And so you know," she went on in the next rest period, "I was foolish and shallow once about looks." She paused and tracked a gaze full of carnal craving across his face. "But, sweetie, that stupidity has sunk to the bottom of the sea." She pressed close to him, and murmured in a husky breath, "Right now, all I want to see is all of you from the waist up," she reached down and undid his belt buckle, "and from the waist down, without a single stitch of clothing. And you'd better have the lights on because I'm a girl who likes to brand a fine image like yours in her mind."

Elizabeth squealed as her husband swept her up in his arms and sprinted for their bedroom. When the door slammed behind them, there was a whole lot of squealing and giggling and heavy breathing followed by two high-pitched sopranos and then silence…at least for a while.

CHAPTER XIV

"OMG, Mom! It's working!"

At Azalea's exclamation, Sonja Love almost dropped the dish of macaroni and cheese she removed from the oven. She set it carefully on the counter and glanced over at her excited fourteen year old, dancing from one foot to the other, a big smile plastered across her cute face. Everybody said Azalea looked like her. *She should*, Sonja thought. *I labored as many hours as her current age to bring her into the world.* "What are you so excited about?" she asked, removing the oven mitts and storing them in a drawer.

"The gym is paying off," Azalea said, moving towards her. "You're smaller here," she touched her mother's hips, "and here." She touched her waist. "Your butt's tighter, too," she complimented her.

"Oh, baby, thank you," Sonja said feelingly, enfolding her in a hug, grateful that *somebody* in this house had noticed. *That* man who sat on the couch watching the T.V. seemed like he was living in perpetual darkness.

"Come here," Azalea commanded, grabbing her hand and tugging her around the wall separating the family room from the kitchen.

"Daddy, Daddy," she said as soon as they entered the family room. "Look at mommy."

"Azalea, I'm trying to listen to the evening news, honey," Terence, said without looking away from the T.V.

His daughter snatched the remote from his lap and froze the frame. "Now, look at her," she commanded sassily.

Reluctantly, Terence turned his gaze to his wife, seeing her plus size and disdaining it inwardly. "I see, Azalea. What's your point?"

His daughter stared at him like he was blind and stupid. In her mind, Sonja thought he was, but she kept quiet, hurt at the indifferent way he'd looked at her and his detached question to their daughter. "She lost weight dad and she looks great!" the teenager exclaimed. "Aren't you happy for her? Mom, who doesn't like exercise, got on a program, stayed on, and lost weight. I think she at least deserves an amen."

Sonja grinned at Azalea's remark and Terence gave a thin smile. With a tepid 'amen,' he turned back to the television.

Azalea rolled her eyes and said, "Come on mom, let's go. Dinner's ready, right?"

"Yes, baby."

"Okay, I'll get Rose and Dahlia."

***

Later that night, Azalea waited until her mother was reading a story to six-year-old Rose before approaching her father. She knocked on her parents' bedroom door.

"Come in," her dad called.

She pushed the door open. He was sitting in bed reading. "Dad, can I talk to you?"

"Sure, honey." He set the book aside and removed his reading glasses.

Azalea closed the door and walked to the edge of the bed. "I don't want mom to hear this, so I'll be quick because I don't know the length of the story she's reading to Rose."

Her father's eyes widened at her frank introduction.

"The Bible says that a man who doesn't look after his family is worse than an infidel. We talked about that in Sabbath School last Saturday at church. A lot of people think that means he's an infidel or terrible person, I guess, if he doesn't support his family financially. But I think that if a man doesn't meet the emotional needs of his family, he is an infidel, a terrible person."

"What are you saying?" Terence asked, feeling like she was calling him an infidel without outright saying so.

"Dad, you need to be more sensitive to mom. She is your wife and you need to respect and love her."

"Now wait one minute, young lady. How dare you come in here and lecture me?"

Azalea had been planning this talk for a while and she was not going to let her father's size, his age, or the plain fact that he was her dad stop her from saying her piece.

"I'm not lecturing you, Dad. I'm telling you something you need to hear so that you can do the right thing. Now please let me finish."

Still looking angry, Terence shut up, nevertheless, and let his daughter speak.

"Now, we all know that mom is overweight, and I know, as well as she, that you don't like it. She has been trying to lose weight, Dad, and I think that when she shows some results, the least you can do is congratulate and encourage her."

"I never noticed until you mentioned it."

"That's probably because you hardly look at her these days or when you do, you don't look for positive things."

Terence narrowed his eyes at his daughter. "What are you trying to say?" He had a feeling she had a great deal of information in that smart brain of hers and was letting only so much out.

"You criticize mom; you don't compliment her."

"I'm not a hypocrite. I don't flatter people."

"It's okay to flatter your wife. You love her so you're supposed to."

Terence had enough. "Azalea, you are only fourteen years old and getting into business way above your age level. Now, you spoke and I heard you. I'll try to be more mindful of your mom's weight loss accomplishments, but it's hard when they are insignificant."

"If you're interested in somebody, you notice things about them."

He gave her a sharp look. "You don't think I'm interested in your mom?"

"You tell me. Are you?" She arched her eyebrows and watched him with an attitude.

"Azalea, I think you've crossed the respect line, so I'll say goodnight."

"I don't think I have, but I apologize if you feel that way. And since you brought up respect, then you need to respect mom and pay attention only to her, rather than to another woman."

"Azalea Florence Love! How dare you?!" her father thundered.

"Don't get angry. You know you keep watching Elizabeth Jones every Sabbath like you don't know that she's married and so are you."

"Young lady, you are not too old to get a spanking."

"Oh, so you want to spank me for telling the truth?"

"What is going on here? Why are you threatening to spank Azalea?" Sonja demanded, opening the door and walking in.

Both her daughter and her husband kept quiet.

"Oh, I just came to tell daddy 'goodnight' and we had a little disagreement, but we're cool now." She bent and kissed Terence's cheek. "I love you, Daddy," she said loud enough for her mother to hear. Beneath her breath she added, "I'm watching you, Dad. Be good. God's watching, also."

She left the room with her father staring after her in consternation and her mother following her exit with a thoughtful expression.

CHAPTER XV

The following day at Mountain Spring General Hospital...

"May I sit here?"

Sonja's heart jerked and her eyes sprinted upwards at the sound of a voice that rumbled like thunder on distant hills. Rick Harrigan. The orderly from the orthopedic unit had been showing up at her lunch hour and lunch table for the past month. Terence was ripped and fit, but nothing like this. Rick looked like he lifted Semi's in his spare time. His muscles and flat abdomen didn't yield in any place Sonja could see to flab. He needed special made scrubs from the uniform factory. The ones he wore fit snugly, not that the female workers minded with the attention he attracted from the simple process of walking from one side of the cafeteria to the next.

"Sure," she answered his question, waving at the vacant chair at her table. He set his tray down and sat.

"How are you, Sonja?" he asked with a smile, unwrapping the Turkey sub and popping the cap on the can of Sprite. "I missed you yesterday."

Sonja concentrated on the remains of her salad trying to deny the curl of pleasure that she felt at a man like this noticing her absence. "It was my day off," she explained.

"It wasn't any fun eating lunch by myself."

"I'm sure you didn't, not with so many willing lunch companions around." She cast a pointed glance around the cafeteria.

He grinned. "You got me. I didn't. I had company, but it wasn't the same."

Sonja arched a brow. "What wasn't the same?"

"Sharing a table with somebody other than you."

She heard the flirtation in his voice and saw playfulness in his look. Sonja told herself that she should shut him down because she was a married woman, although he didn't know it since she didn't wear a ring. But his interest fed an emptiness inside her that her husband wouldn't fill. Besides, it was harmless, so she responded to it like she had been doing for the past two weeks. She sipped her punch and fluttered her lashes a little. "You mean the conversation wasn't stimulating?"

"Now there's a word," he said.

The husky rumble of his voice worked the sensitive areas of her skin that had been neglected too long.

"It wasn't the conversation that wasn't stimulating; it was the people."

"Oh," she said, understanding from his pointed stare that he found her stimulating.

"You changed your hair," he observed, changing the topic. "It's pretty."

"Thanks." She almost preened, glad he'd noticed. Terence hadn't said a thing. The adjustment in the style had been subtle, full bangs versus side-swept ones, but he hadn't noticed. Rick did.

"Listen, do you ever get tired of the food in the caf?" he asked.

"Sometimes, but I make my own lunch when that happens."

"How about we go off site one day?"

At this point, she should have said 'no thanks, I can't' or 'thanks, but I'm married and I can't.' But words emerged that Sonja refused to admit were pre-meditated. "That would be nice."

"How about tomorrow?"

Another chance to do the right thing; she didn't take it.

"Sounds good," she agreed, her heart knocking with equal parts excitement and trepidation.

***

"Man, I haven't seen you in over a month. I thought you quit morning workouts."

"I switched to night workouts for a while," Isaac answered Terence with a secret smile. The activities he and Elizabeth indulged in at nights and into the early hours of the morning wore him out. He hadn't been able to rouse himself to get to the gym at five-thirty. Now he was trying to get back on the program; he'd have to see how long it would last, because his wife was unpredictable when it came to intimacy. She seemed to enjoy rousing him in more ways than just wakefulness when she caught a mood, which tended to be two or three o'clock in the morning. At five a.m., he was usually falling back to sleep.

"Hey," Terence called, slowing down the treadmill as Isaac picked up his pace. "What's that sly smile I see?"

Isaac began to grin outright. He slowed the speed on his machine to a slow walk. "This one you mean?" he asked, showing Terence all his brace-perfected whites.

"Yeah, that one. What's going on?"

"Elizabeth and I made up." The words shot out of his mouth with all of the joy he felt since that happened. He didn't notice Terence's silence. "The day we spoke and I told you all the problems, she made me dinner and we made up. Things have been great ever since."

I just bet they are, Terence thought sourly, managing a smile that nearly broke both jaws and consumed what little energy the workout left behind. For the next five minutes, he listened to Isaac go on about how good God was, how great forgiveness felt, and what a wonderful woman God had blessed him with. At the end of the monologue, he thought, jealousy eating at him, *you won't feel so blessed by this afternoon.*

He borrowed Isaac's phone before they left the gym, since he'd left his in the car...not quite.

CHAPTER XVI

Elizabeth was so excited that she could barely contain herself. She couldn't stop praising God, and she suspected Karen and Adrianna had stopped answering her calls because they were sick of hearing her say the same thing over and over again, "I'm so happy that I don't know what to do with myself."

She was in her second trimester of pregnancy. Morning sickness was long gone. Her last medical check revealed that the pregnancy was progressing normally, and the baby was developing as it should. At her invitation, Isaac had come with her to her last prenatal visit. When he heard the baby's heartbeat on the fetal Doppler, the expression of wonder on his face was something Liz would remember for keeps. That evening, about three days ago, he'd gotten on his knees before her and begged her forgiveness for refusing to claim a child that was a precious part of her. Would she consider accepting him as the father for her baby? Tears in her eyes, Elizabeth knelt with him and told him that there was no other father for this child but him, and this baby was *their* baby not hers. That night, their lovemaking had taken on a new dimension of tenderness, and Elizabeth felt her love deepen for her husband.

From the time on her Movado, she had twenty minutes to make the date with Isaac. Elizabeth grinned like a fool as she remembered the text she'd gotten this morning, inviting her on this date. Like she had been doing since she first read the text, she checked the message on her iPhone again. It had come in at six a.m. this morning: *Hi, baby, Just finished my work out and thought of you. Meet me for Lunch at*

Selena's? One o'clock. Love you. She picked it up after he left for work and thought him suave and creative that he didn't say anything. She confirmed the date.

Elizabeth was so excited that her hand shook as she applied eyeliner. She nearly stuck herself in the eye. She didn't wear make-up much, but today she wanted to look alluring and sexier than Isaac had ever seen her. With her tummy protruding now, marking her an obviously pregnant woman, Elizabeth figured she'd use all the help she could get. When she finished her ensemble, she scrutinized her reflection in the mirror and thought she looked elegant, even with her expanded waistline. In a v-neck lemon-colored sweater and low rider stretch maternity jeans, she was attractive. She twisted her head from side to side and fidgeted with her curls. Recently, she put a rinse in, changing her jet black strands to brunette. Isaac liked it as well as the shorter style she'd gone with. Elizabeth grabbed her purse and keys and hurried out the door to her date.

***

Five minutes before he left his office, Isaac picked up Elizabeth's email, telling him that she couldn't make it because of an emergency staff teleconference with one of the colleges she worked for. Disappointment danced through him; he'd been looking forward to seeing his wife. He hated leaving her at home in the mornings and left work on time, often working through his lunch hour to meet his daily design deadlines, so that he could leave on time at five o'clock to spend his evenings with her. Now, the lunch he'd been looking forward to was off the table. He grimaced and resigned himself to rushing downstairs to the food court to grab a sandwich. When his cell phone rang he answered absently, his mind on Elizabeth and the lunch he'd been looking forward to.

"Hey, Isaac, had lunch already?"

"Terence?" Isaac questioned, surprised at the unexpected call and at this time of the day. Usually, Terence was busy at Mountain Springs' emergency call center.

"That's me," he confirmed. "Listen, I'm off today and wondered if you'd like to grab some lunch with me. I'm buying."

"Sure, why not?" He agreed and then joked with Terence that he was a poor replacement for the date with his wife.

Terence laughed and they agreed to meet at Selena's.

***

Elizabeth sat at a corner table in Selena's, sipping lemonade and waiting for her husband to show up. She checked the mirror in her purse and thought that her liner enhanced eyes made her sultry, and the glittered cherry gloss she wore called attention to her lips and hopefully would tease her hubby into kissing her. She felt like a girl on a first date, like ants were in her pants, and she couldn't keep still. Her eagerness made it hard to believe that she'd seen him a mere four hours ago. Elizabeth understood that love, the real deal, made a woman feel like that about her man. She smiled and sipped more lemonade.

"Elizabeth?"

Her eyes travelled a long distance to the face of the man who spoke her name. Model or actor? His face fit both professions. Cinnamon brown and smooth, his skin had a polished glow that garnered attention and generated stares from females. Handsome, yes, and Liz did not deny it even though she was happily married. His shoulders, the breadth of them, had lean-on-me-when-you-feel-weak written all over them. The guy smiled down at her with teeth so white and straight that she knew only cosmetic dental surgery could achieve that type of perfection. Beyond his beauty, Elizabeth saw the bouquet of red roses at the same time that he extended them to her. "These are for you," he announced, the husky timber of his voice designed for nights on the oceanfront with intoxication high and inhibitions low. Liz blinked, catching an image that, thank God, involved her and her husband on the ocean front, not her and this guy. The romantic ballad she heard in her imagination eased into reality, and Elizabeth realized that a stranger was singing her lines from the Lionel Richie love song, "Three Times a Lady."

It was one of her favorites. How did he know? Who was he? As he sang, leaning close, she heard the hush in the restaurant and figured everybody was watching and listening. Embarrassed, she opened her mouth to ask questions, but he silenced her with a forefinger to his lips.

Elizabeth took the card he extended, read his name on the front, Nick Warren, and flipped it over when he motioned for her to do so. The message on the back read, *From me to you sweetheart. So, sorry I can't make lunch. Love you. Hope this song keeps you until dinner. Love Isaac.*

86

Her hand was over her heart and Elizabeth, along with every other woman in Selena's, was fighting tears by the time Nick Warren wound down the 1980's ballad.

"Thank you so much," she said, giving him a shaky smile through her tears. She blinked and didn't dare dab at her eyes before she messed up her liner.

"You're welcome," the guy responded. "He also asked me to do this." He lifted her hand and placed a gentle kiss on it. When he leaned close and placed a quick kiss on her cheek, the place erupted with applause. "You're very lucky," he murmured, continuing to lean close to a completely off-kilter and totally flabbergasted Liz. "Not a lot of men love their wives this much anymore."

***

Elizabeth fell asleep on the sofa waiting for Isaac to come home. When she opened her eyes, the house was quiet as if she were the only one there. She pushed herself upright and squinted into the pale glow of light from the lamps on either side of the sofa. The chill from the fall night had seeped into the house, and into the leather of the cushions. Elizabeth felt the coldness of the seat beneath her palms. What time was it? She checked the face of her watch. Ten o'clock. Where was Isaac? He hadn't answered any of her multiple calls, hadn't returned any of them, and hadn't responded to her texts. After the spectacular serenade he'd arranged for her, at least he could have called to ensure that everything went well.

She got up and headed for the bathroom, starting to worry about her husband. As far as she knew, he planned to come home at the usual time, which was six o'clock. Where was he? Elizabeth entered the bathroom, relieved her bladder, and washed her hands, wondering what to do and who to call. His office wasn't open now, so that didn't make sense. Earlier when she had called, the receptionist had said he was engaged and took a message. She hadn't wanted to bother him again since he was busy.

Liz turned off the bathroom light and used the interconnecting door to enter her bedroom, thinking about calling her sisters to enlist their help and get some advice about finding her missing husband. Bright light illuminated the room, and Elizabeth's finger stayed stuck to the switch at the sight of Isaac fast asleep in their bed. When had he come home? And why hadn't he called her?

The sudden brilliance woke him up. He squinted, shielded his eyes, and sat up. "Why's the light on?" he asked, his voice raspy with sleep.

"Why's the light on?" Elizabeth echoed, her incredulity feeling like it was turning into irritation. "Why didn't you tell me you were home?"

"Liz, I'm tired. All I want to do right now is sleep." He flopped back down turned on his stomach and stuck his head beneath his pillow.

Elizabeth got mad. First, he'd been a no-show at lunch. Granted he'd cushioned the disappointment with the flowers and the song, but he hadn't called afterwards. Now he'd come into the house and hadn't had the decency to tell her he was home. To top off his neglect and lack of consideration, he ignored her question about his peculiar, not to mention, rude action.

Elizabeth marched to the side of the bed and snatched the pillow from his head. "Isaac Jones, I asked you a question, and I want an answer," she commanded.

He stayed inert, not saying a single word.

"Did you hear me?" she demanded, raising her voice. "I called you all day and left messages, which you didn't answer. I waited up for you, and you come home and didn't have the consideration to wake me up to let me know you were here. What is going on?"

He shot off the bed and got in her face so fast that Elizabeth stumbled back in surprise. She took another step back at the menace and fury in his countenance. *What in the Lord's name?*

"Don't you dare play innocent with me because you are NOT!"

She searched his face in bewilderment, at a loss as to what she was guilty of. "Wha—" she began, but he interrupted her.

"You told me you wanted to meet at Selena's today, and then you email me to say that you can't because you have a meeting. Then when I show up there for lunch anyway, you're there letting some man paw and kiss you and give you flowers."

Elizabeth started shaking her head from the time he talked about email. "I didn't sen—"

"DON'T lie to me Elizabeth!"

He hadn't even let her finish before he concluded that she was lying.

"Who was that man? Is he the man you're pregnant for?"

"No!" she exclaimed aghast at his far-fetched conclusion.

"You're lying!" he shouted. "You promised me that from the time we made up our relationship would be based on honesty. But the first chance you get, you reconnect with your lover. What was it?" he demanded, moving close as Elizabeth stepped back, shrinking from the venom in his face and the wild look in his eyes. "Did he call you, and you dropped me, cancelled our date so that you could be with him?

"No," she denied, still backing away. "I did—"

"Is that it, Liz?" he interrupted her again. "Is that what you did?" He went on, his voice low, harsh, and threatening.

She shook her head, knowing with the rage rolling off him like heat, he wasn't registering her negatives.

"IS IT?" he roared.

Elizabeth jumped, "N-no," she managed, frightened by his out-of-control behavior.

"Liar," he snarled, raising fists coiled so tightly that the skin stretched to the breaking point across his knuckles.

Elizabeth held her breath, not knowing from his crazy behavior if he would hit her.

He breathed hard and swung away from her, and she almost slid down the wall, limp with relief.

"You said you called me, all day," he started up again, swinging to face her. His scorn-filled glance made her feel like vermin recently escaped from sewage.

"If you didn't hear from me, why didn't you come to my office to check on me if you were so concerned or wanted to see me so much?"

Elizabeth had thought about it, but when the receptionist said he was engaged, she hadn't wanted to disturb his work. She opened her mouth to explain, but again he didn't let her.

"I'll tell you why you didn't come," he said, his voice thick and unpleasant. "You were occupied with your lover all day, and you ran home before I came so you could pretend to wait for me. But what you didn't know was that I already saw you making out with him in public."

He slapped the heel of his palm to his forehead. "Why in heaven's name did I believe you? Why did I ever trust your words? It's impossible for you to tell the truth." He swung back to her, his eyes blazing even more than before with anger as he talked. "You're a lying, cheating woman who couldn't be honest if your life were on the line. But what did I expect from a slut like you?"

Elizabeth gasped at the insult, shocked that he'd labeled her with that vulgar word. But he wasn't done yet. He went on, while she tried to catch breath from the denigration.

"You have no morals, no heart, and no conscience. That's why you slept with a married man, and that's why you tried to pass off this pregnancy on an unsuspecting, gullible, head-over-heels-in-love-with-you idiot," he jabbed his thumb into his chest in self-mockery, "me. It's why you let him handle and fondle and do only God knows what else to you today—because you're loose, because you're wonton, because you're addicted to sex, because you are a whore!"

He should have stopped at slut. Shaking with an emotion on the far opposite side of fear now, Elizabeth pushed off the wall, no longer needing its support to keep her upright. The righteous anger welling up inside snapped her spine erect. She stood at her full five-feet-ten inches barefoot height trembling with the ultimate insult to her womanhood, and from her husband no less.

"I SWEAR," she spat, pushing her face right into his, "that if you malign me with ONE MORE derogatory word, I will clock you so hard, you'll need surgery to get your head back on straight."

Shocked at her switch from cowering to combative, Isaac stood there and stared at her. Now that she'd shut him up, Elizabeth started talking. "First of all, I didn't send you an email canceling our date. The man you saw singing to me and giv—"

"I saw him in your personal space, kissing you, and touching you," he bit out.

"Isaac," she said calmly, "please let me finish."

"Liz, I don't want to hear any lies that you manufactured to cover up your wrong. I'm beyond gullibility," he said wearily, sitting down at the edge of the bed as if he were truly tired.

She sat beside him. "How about listening to the truth?"

He braced his elbows on his knees, and dropped his forehead into his hands. "How will I know it's the truth?"

"You'll know because I promised to tell you the truth."

"Liz, right now your word is shaky and that's putting it nicely."

"Isaac, look at me," she commanded. Elizabeth turned sideways and folded a leg beneath her so that she could face him. He didn't budge. "Isaac, look at me, please," she asked, tugging at his hand. When he didn't cooperate, she changed tactics and went to her knees before him. She shoved his legs apart, dislodging his elbows.

"What are you doing?" he asked frowning and staring at her as if he thought she was crazy.

"Trying to get through to you," she said, scooting between his legs and getting into his personal space. He leaned back a bit, watching her. Now that she had his full attention, she rested her palms on his thighs and started explaining. "Like I was saying. I didn't cancel the date through email or any other means. This guy you saw, Nick Warren he said his name was, came up to me while I was waiting for you. He offered me the flowers and a note from you telling me that you were the one who sent him. You couldn't make the date so you sent him with the serenade. The kiss and up-close part that you saw were a part of his job..." she trailed off at the vehement shaking of Isaac's head.

"I didn't send that guy," Isaac denied.

"Then who did?"

He lifted his shoulders, as clueless as she.

Elizabeth rubbed her forehead, thinking. "Which email did that message come from—the one canceling the date?"

"From your Gmail."

She couldn't remember ever giving anybody access to that account. She rubbed her forehead harder, thinking deeper. The clarity that she needed came, and then Liz didn't want it anymore. *Oh dear, Lord!*

She pushed away from her husband and grabbed her phone from the nightstand. Disconnecting it from the charger, she entered her passcode and checked the day's messages. She scrolled to the one from her husband inviting her on the date. It was from his phone. For a moment there she thought, it might be from elsewhere. Resuming her kneeling position before Isaac, she shook her head, baffled. "I didn't send that message even though it came from my mail," she told him.

"Then somebody has your password."

She nodded, not ready to reveal the suspect she had in mind. "Something strange is going on. Think about this: You texted me this morning, inviting me on the date. I texted back and accepted. Why would I then email you to cancel it? The easiest way was to have kept the texts going." Elizabeth watched him and saw that he was considering her logic. His thick brows met over the bridge of his nose, and he folded his bottom lip inwards as he thought.

Elizabeth found him endearing when he did that. She couldn't resist. She leaned in and startled him with a kiss.

"Why'd you do that?"

"Because you're cute and I can't help myself."

That pulled a smile from him, and then he shocked her with his next remark. "I didn't text you to invite you on a date."

"You didn't?" Liz asked, taken aback. "But I have it right here." She showed him the text he'd sent to her around six a.m. this morning.

"That's strange. I didn't send that." He plucked his phone from the side of his briefcase, entered his code and showed her his messages from her phone. "See, the first text is you telling me *Ok, it's a date. Selena's at 1 it is.* Nothing before that."

"So who sent me this text?" she gestured at the screen of her device.

"Beats me."

Elizabeth stared at her phone with narrowed eyes. "I don't like this," she told Isaac. She asked him something that had been bothering her from one of his earlier statements. "You said you came to Selena's, although I'd canceled the date. Why?" The hardwood was starting to bruise her knees. She got up and perched her behind on her husband's right leg. His arm automatically circled her waist. When his palm spread on her belly, Elizabeth felt as if he surrounded her as well as the baby with his protection.

"You make it hard to stay angry with you," he mumbled, wrapping his other hand around her and settling her more comfortably on his leg.

"I know," she said and kissed him. "Now, why did you come to Selena's?"

"To have lunch with my friend, Terence."

Elizabeth stiffened. *Please God, please not Terence Love.* "Terence? Who's that?" she asked casually.

"Terence, you know the deacon from church."

"Terence Love?" The words struggled out of her throat and touched the air in a hush.

"Yes, him. He called me up and invited me to lunch at Selena's.

Since you cancelled the date, rather, since our date was cancelled, I went."

"And that's how you saw this guy kissing me," Elizabeth said quietly, things beginning to fall into place, an ugly picture of mischief becoming clear.

"Right."

"Is Terence a friend of yours?" she asked, hoping that the man wasn't.

"We work out at McBride's together in the mornings. I guess you could say we're friends, more like gym buddies, though. We've shot a few hoops together on Sundays. Today was the first time we had lunch together."

And it will be your last.

"I didn't see you come into Selena's."

"I didn't. I was upset by what I saw through the window. Terence and I went to Brandy's over on Market Street."

Elizabeth looped an arm around Isaac's shoulders and rested her cheek next to his. Molasses and spice: Him and Her. That's what they were, or so they appeared from their reflections in the mirror, hanging on the wall across from them. "I love you, Isaac," she said softly, wanting him to hear it, and, more than that, to know it before she revealed her final secret to him. He needed to know that the man he thought a friend was really his mortal enemy. "Isaac, I have to tell you something."

"Liz, before you do that, I need to say something."

She pulled slightly away from him so she could see him better. Elizabeth watched his small eyes turn regretful as he spoke his next words.

"Liz, I behaved like a first class jackass a short while ago, and I want to apologize for going off on you the way I did. It doesn't matter that I thought you'd betrayed me, I shouldn't have acted that way. More than that, I should never have used the words I did." He swallowed and dropped his gaze from before her steady one, ashamed of the names he'd called her. "It was disrespectful, and cruel, and low. I was angry, which is no excuse. I don't see you that way." He stopped again and raised a halting gaze to meet hers. "I guess I'm still fighting to believe that a woman as beautiful as you really loves me. I was jealous of the thought that another man had your affections. It tore me up and made me crazy to think that you didn't care about me. Liz, I know the words might sound meaningless when the weight and ugliness of the despicable ones I spoke still echo in the air. But I want you to know that I do love you, and I'll not make that mistake again to disrespect you like that. Thank you, for shutting me down the way you did."

Elizabeth leaned close and brushed her nose across her husband's. She kissed his eyelids, his nose, and then his mouth. "I think that is the humblest and most believable apology I've ever heard, and I accept it."

"Thank you, Liz," he said, squeezing her closer.

"Now, I have something to tell you and I need for you to hold me even closer than you're doing now."

He pulled her more snugly into his arms. "How's this?" he asked, his hands occupied with more than hugging—one hand actively caressing her right hip.

"Good," Liz smiled. "I feel the love." She took a deep breath. "Terence is not your friend. In fact, I think he's the one who orchestrated this date to create mischief between us."

"Why would he do that?" Isaac asked in confusion.

"To break us up. He wants me back."

Elizabeth thought she heard the low hum of the refrigerator in the silence that followed.

"He-He's the guy?" Isaac asked, sounding like he was going to faint.

She nodded.

"He's the married guy, the one who…" he trailed off and touched her belly. Unsaid, but loud and clear was that Terence Love was their baby's biological father.

Elizabeth nodded again, and her husband fell silent once more. She said nothing, giving him time to work through the land mine of information that had just detonated.

"Does he know?" he finally asked, his voice rough with an emotion that Elizabeth couldn't identify.

She shook her head. "I didn't tell him."

"Good," Isaac said, drawing her tighter into his embrace. "I'm glad you didn't. This baby is mine, and he'll *never* take it or you away from me."

Those were the sweetest words Elizabeth had ever heard from her husband. "Isaac Jones," she said, "I sincerely love you with all my heart and all my soul." When their lips met, the kiss endured well into the night.

CHAPTER XVII

"How you doing, man?"

Ninety-five. Isaac kept count in his head, ignoring Terence and pacing his breathing as he did overhead presses. His muscles bunching, he pushed up on the barbell again defying one hundred pounds of weights, fifty on each side, to stop him. *Ninety-six. Only four to go.* He blinked sweat from his eyes and stayed with it. *Ninety-seven.*

"What happened last night?"

Isaac held his focus, feeling a burn from more than exercise, but fighting to control it. Up. *Ninety-eight.* Down. *Two to go now.* Up. *Ninety-nine.* Down.

"You okay?"

"One hundred," Isaac panted aloud and brought the barbell down for the final time. He stepped away from the stand, and paid attention to Terence for the first time since the man spoke to him. "Why?" he answered Terence with a question. "Did you think I wouldn't be?" he asked coolly, taking a swig from his water bottle.

The man pulled back a little, no doubt startled by his tone. "No." Terence laughed uncertainly. "With what you saw yesterday, I wondered how things went with your wife last night, that's all."

Wiping sweat from his face with his towel in slow and deliberate movements, he took his time answering Terence, all the while watching the predator, who unknown to him until last night, meant him no good all this time. "You saw what I saw, how do you think it went?" He settled a steady stare on the man, and as Terence shifted, letting his eyes slither away like the snake that he was, Isaac saw his nervousness. *Home wrecker. Wife stealer. Bastard—such a good word, but a pity I can't say it aloud.*

"Not good," Terence answered with a nervous laugh.

"But that was the plan all along wasn't it?" Isaac said calmly, his unexpected statement catching the man off-guard.

Terence's expression floundered between consternation and confusion. "Plan? What plan?" he asked continuing to pretend, while his gaze jumped all over the weight room as if seeking an escape route.

"You know, the one to break me and Liz up," he said casually, draping the towel around his neck and holding onto either end.

"I don't know what you're talking about," the man denied, but he sounded and looked guiltier than a kid caught with a hand in the proverbial cookie jar.

"I think you do, Terence," Isaac contradicted, controlling his temper so he wouldn't go off on this scoundrel who'd caused him to verbally abuse his wife last night and almost lose her. The memory of his violence then and the sting of its shame also held him in check.

"Why would you think that?" His forced laugh was as fake as his attempt to appear clueless.

"Because you borrowed my phone yesterday morning, and Liz got a text from it about a date with me at Selena's at the time you had it. Because I got an email from her, one she never sent, cancelling the date. Because it's more than odd that, out of the blue, you called to suggest we have lunch at Selena's. And it's real fishy that we got there right in time to see some singer kiss her—a singer whom I never sent to serenade my wife."

"Why would I get involved in your business like that?" he blustered, still contriving innocence, even though the handwriting was on the wall where his guilt was concerned.

"Why don't you stop acting like an ass?" Isaac snapped in disgust. "You're guilty as hell and you know it."

"Isaac, man. You and I have been buddies. I never sent any emails."

And your sins will expose you. Didn't the Bible say something like that in the Numbers 32:23?

"I never accused you of sending any. I said, I got an email from my wife, one she never sent."

Terence's mouth opened and closed without a sound emerging. He finally shut it and started pinching his nose.

Busted wide open. Isaac was done with his workout and done with this guy.

"Let me tell you something, Terence. Whatever my wife had with you is over. I've got her now, and I'm not giving her up. We love each other, so the battle you're fighting is useless. The dirty trick you pulled yesterday didn't work and never will because our love can't be broken. Stop wasting your time on us and go work on your own marriage." Without sparing Terence another glance, Isaac got his water bottle and turned towards the exit.

"You can't satisfy her," Terence snarled. "You can't even knock her up. I did that."

Isaac whirled and drove his fist right into Terence's mouth. The man stumbled backwards and sat down hard on a weight bench. Exertion aborted around them, along with the heavy breathing that went with it. Every guy stopped his work out to watch.

Terence wiped the trickle of blood from the corner of his lip. Hatred in his gaze he practically bellowed, "You can't even get it up."

Isaac socked him two fast ones—one to the mouth and the other to his right eye, knocking him flat on his back unto the bench. He hit it at an angle and tumbled to the side ending up with a leg draped over the bench and his upper body partially on the floor. Somebody heralded, "Fiiiiiiight," and that was all it took for a testosterone filled room to take up the chant, "Fight, fight, fight."

Jim McBride, Mac, showed up as Terence gained his feet. "Okay, okay, break it up," he said, stepping between them. "You guys know better. Take it outside, please." He sent them each a warning look.

Isaac gave him a clipped nod of understanding and headed for the locker room to get his things. As he walked away, he heard Terence complain, "He started it, Mac."

"No, *you* did," Bobby Jean, a guy who had been two weight benches away from them accused.

The weight room's automatic door slid shut behind him and silenced Terence's reply.

In the locker room, Isaac changed his shorts and stepped wearily into his sweat pants, adrenalin rush settling into exhaustion. His phone rang, and adrenalin shot through the roof at Elizabeth's hysterical sobs and screams.

"Liz! Liz!" He raised his voice above her screeches. "I can't hear you clearly. What're you losing?"

"Our baby! I'm bleeding."

Dear God! "Did you call the doctor?" He asked urgently, shrugging into his sweatshirt, grabbing his bag and running for the exit.

"S-She told m-me to go to the h-hospital, but I'm scared to drive. Honey, please come."

"I'm on my way, Liz, but how bad is it? Maybe you should call an ambulance."

In the SUV now, he scrabbled to get the key in the ignition, and it fell from his shaking fingers to the floor.

"No, I want you with me. Come, just come, please."

"I'll be there in five minutes," he promised.

***

Elizabeth disconnected the call, resorting to incoherent prayers, but trusting that God understood the jumble. Isaac had asked how bad the bleeding was and she deliberately hadn't answered because she didn't want him to have an accident getting here. It was bad, like the flooding common on day two of her menstrual cycle. Nobody had to tell her that it wasn't a propitious sign for a pregnant woman. Spotting was a bad sign in pregnancy. Full-blown bleeding like this was critical. She woke up to use the bathroom and discovered that her wet undergarment wasn't as a result of the bladder release dream but vaginal bleeding. She'd called the doctor who immediately ordered her to the hospital. She called Isaac because she needed him to take her. She thought about calling an ambulance, but she was scared and wanted her husband by her side. The gym wasn't far away. Elizabeth was frightened about what this bleeding meant, and she wanted someone who could calm and comfort her and give her reassurance. Isaac Jones, her husband, was the only one who fit the bill. *Come, Isaac, please come now*, she whispered in her head, closing her eyes tightly and praying harder as she felt another rush of warm liquid flood out of her womb.

CHAPTER XVIII

Dr. Fields was at the hospital when they arrived. Elizabeth tried to pull calm from the doctor's serenity and strength from her husband's firm grasp.

"Am I losing my baby, doctor?" she asked, expecting a miracle from the woman even though she hadn't yet done an examination.

"Let's not panic yet," Dr. Fields soothed, her voice relaxed and comforting. She pulled on gloves and folded back the sheet the nurse had draped over Elizabeth. "I want to take a look at the blood flow to determine how heavy it is."

Elizabeth closed her eyes as the doctor looked, and she heard Isaac breathe out a shaky "Jesus, Oh Jesus." Her eyes flew open and she saw him watching her pelvis with a fixed horror. From what she'd seen earlier and the warm rush she had been feeling down there, she knew the picture wasn't pretty.

"We'll need to do a fetal monitoring and an ultrasound immediately, Elizabeth. Afterwards, I'll do a pelvic check."

"What do you think is causing that, doctor?" Isaac asked hoarsely, gesturing in the direction of his wife's vaginal area.

To Elizabeth, Dr. Fields's smile seemed forced. "I'm not sure, which is why we have to do the monitoring and ultrasound," the woman hedged.

"But in your experience, what could cause something like this?" Isaac pressed hearing the caginess in her voice.

She summoned the nurse before answering. "It's possible that this is a placental abruption."

"What's that?"

Dr. Fields gave rapid instructions to the nurse, and then replied, "That's a situation where the placenta separates partially or completely from the uterus prior to delivery. But," she raised her hand when Isaac opened his mouth again, "we don't know if that is what this is."

"That sounds very bad for the baby," he said.

"It can deprive the fetus of oxygen, so, yes, it is serious." She smiled grimly and turned to Elizabeth, who'd started feeling faint from the frightening conversation. "Some orderlies are coming to wheel you over to one of the two OB Emergency rooms. Let me ask you some quick questions. Over the past few days, have you had any uterine tenderness or soreness or any back pain?"

"Yesterday, my back was hurting quite a bit," Elizabeth admitted.

"No uterine tenderness?"

Elizabeth shook her head.

"Remember we talked about quickening before, the first signs of your baby moving. It happens between sixteen and twenty-five weeks. At twenty weeks, like you are now, you might have felt something like flutters in your stomach, quickening. Did you notice anything like that?"

"Last week, I thought I felt something, but it was so fast and faint that I wasn't sure."

"And you haven't felt anything more recently like yesterday or today?"

Elizabeth shook her head. "Why?"

"Just routine questions," the doctor reassured her with a smile as the orderlies arrived.

Elizabeth didn't think that it was routine at all. She gripped Isaac's hand more firmly as her heart began to really pound with fear of an outcome that seemed inevitable, but which she could not bear to think about, much less accept.

***

They didn't hear the usual thudding of the baby's heartbeat via the fetal monitor. Dr. Fields was fighting not to display alarm, but even a dunce could tell that she was disturbed as she moved the probe all over Elizabeth's stomach, trying to get a heartbeat but coming up empty.

101

Isaac's right hand had turned numb from the circulation restrictive hold that Elizabeth had on it. Neither of them spoke; neither one could— she due to the silent tears rolling down her cheeks, and he because of the mountain of emotion blocking his throat.

"We'll have to do an ultrasound before making a definitive diagnosis," Dr. Fields said quietly, and proceeded to do that when the parents remained mute.

A half hour later, Isaac sat on the edge of the hospital bed, pressing his wife's face against his chest to muffle her screams that were subsiding to moans of agony now.

The diagnosis had come in: Stillbirth at twenty weeks. Their baby had died in utero. Cause of death: Oxygen deprivation due to placental abruption. What caused the abruption? Reason unknown.

Isaac clutched Elizabeth to his chest, squeezing her body close to his and pressing her into him, oblivious to the possibility that he might be hurting her. He hurt so much that holding her this close was the only outlet for his pain. He couldn't scream like she did because one of them had to stay rational. He couldn't bellow his grief out loud because he had to be the strength in their suffering, the solace in their sorrow, and the anchor in their anguish. So he rocked and comforted her, telling her how sorry he was for the loss of their baby. He whispered how much he shared her heartache and how deeply he felt her distress. Isaac promised that, by the grace of God, they would get through this together. He made the promise, wishing all the while that he could replace the child they had lost with a substitute, and knowing that he couldn't now and possibly never would. The tears, suspended behind his lids by force, broke free and ran down his face. Like Hannah of old in Bible times, who asked the Lord in 1 Samuel 1:9-11 to open her barren womb, Isaac silently begged God to spike his stagnant sperm count so that he could give Elizabeth a child.

CHAPTER XIX

They pulled up to the rear entrance of the Elegant Inn in Heart Haven, a neighboring Seneca Mountain Community to Mountain Spring, where Sonja had rented a room for the night. Her family thought she was working a double and wouldn't get off until eleven o'clock tonight. So after work ended at three p.m., she made a reservation at Elegant, changed there, and met Rick for their dinner date, the third one this week.

Dinner done, he brought her back to the hotel. The heavy rumble of the Dodge's custom-built engine died as he twisted the key in the ignition and slowly removed it. Like their previous two dates, Sonja felt sad that the evening was about to close. She watched Rick circle the hood to open her door in the usual way he'd been doing on all their dates. In scrubs he was mouth-watering; in that spandex and Lycra shirt that defined every ridge and plane of muscle on his chest, he was every woman's ideal nightcap.

That word gave Sonja an idea that her conscience told her would end in a broken commandment. She ignored it. At her room's door, they both hesitated. She battled to settle the war between her carnal mind and her conscience. She wasn't sure why he hovered.

"It's been an amazing evening," he said, his voice a low echo that strummed across every one of her acutely-aware-of-him nerves.

"Yes, it has," she agreed in a whisper, gripping the key card to still the nervousness rattling her knuckles against each other.

"I'd like it to continue, but only if you want the same thing."

The ball was squarely in her court now, something she never wanted. Sonja knew what she should do, knew what she should say but the words wouldn't come.

"You're a beautiful woman, Sonja, and I'd love to be with you beyond what's been happening between us."

Making love, he means.

"But I'm not sure it's what you want. I can sense and see the struggle in you. This is supposed to be for our mutual enjoyment, but it won't be like that when you're worried about your husband."

"How did you know?" she gasped, embarrassed that he'd deduced her marital status.

He shrugged and smiled. "You drive to our dates or when I pick you up, as in tonight, it's from a hotel. That tells me you're hiding something. A woman's not covert like that unless she's hiding her date from her husband or the man she's currently with." He brushed a wisp of hair from her cheek. "So tell me, beautiful, who're you hiding me from, your husband or your live-in guy?"

Sonja let out a guilty breath and watched the curling patterns on the wine-colored carpet. "It's my husband," she confessed.

He caught her chin in a gentle grip and tipped her head up, "I know there has to be a problem with him if you're seeing me. I don't want to know what it is. All I want is for you to be happy."

Sincerity shone in his brown eyes and his smile showed genuine concern for her contentment. Her eyes felt peppery with tears at his caring. "With you, I'm happy," she whispered.

"Which is all I need to know," he murmured, lowering his head and covering her mouth in their first kiss.

Starved for intimacy, Sonja responded to his gentle kiss with a passion that flared the kiss to wildfire in a flash. At her hungry and eager response, Rick dispensed with ease of acquaintance and moved to sensual familiarity. Right there in the corridor of the hotel, she yielded to his advance, sucking his probing tongue in like a vacuum and shivering and moaning with pleasure at the sexual excitement strumming through her body from that intimate connection. His hands, as busy as his mouth, moved over her body, slipping down her sides, resting on her hips, and changing direction from downward waltz to sideways shift.

"So full, just the way I like it," he murmured against her lips.

Sonja trembled both from his touch and his words of appreciation.

He kissed her hard, the caress consuming and filled with need. "So much of you to hold. God, I love the feel of you in my arms," he said in a voice roughened by desire when they paused to breathe.

"Not too big?" she asked the hushed question against his lips when they paused to breathe.

"I'm a big guy, Sonja, I don't need a birch in my arms."

"Will an oak do?" she asked, thinking that was the type of tree she resembled with her bulk.

"Every time, so you're perfect."

They didn't talk after that. The kiss that followed brought a shuddering below her waist that she hadn't felt since the last time she was with her husband, and that was a long time ago. When Rick plucked the key card from her fingers and opened the door, she made no protest. When he walked her backwards into the room, she remained silent. When the door clicked closed behind them, it was too late for a change of mind.

***

A month had passed since Elizabeth lost the baby. Although she was going through the motions of living, Isaac could tell she wasn't herself. So could the rest of her family. Everybody was worried about her, but she kept insisting that she was okay. She returned to teaching classes a week after the loss of their son. Isaac suggested grief counseling, but she refused. She told him she was through with tears; if she needed to release more grief, she'd do it on her own. Confessing her pain to a bunch of strangers who'd suffered similar loss would not bring her healing. She'd been extremely vehement about it, so Isaac had let the matter rest.

Now on this Monday evening, he came home from work to find her locked in one of the four bedrooms they had converted into a home office for her. The place was neat and orderly, and he saw a huge bin of folded laundry in one corner of their bedroom. Elizabeth had taken to washing in the wee hours of the morning. Isaac knew she had trouble sleeping and didn't want to take the sleeping pills the doctor had prescribed. She was engaging in a chore she hated at an ungodly hour and she'd just lost a baby. It didn't take genius to realize how traumatized her mind was. She kept herself occupied so she wouldn't go crazy. She'd taken on extra classes, too. He'd found out two weeks ago when he called to take her to lunch. She couldn't go because she had a scheduled teleconference. Isaac was worried that she'd have a nervous breakdown, and had tried to tell her so. She dismissed it with the litany she used with everyone who expressed concern for her near maniacal fixation on work, "I'll be fine." The fact that she used the future tense meant she knew she wasn't yet healed; at least she wasn't in denial about that. Isaac tried to look on the bright side.

Isaac changed into cargos and a T-shirt, and then went in search of his wife. Her office door was closed but not locked. He knocked and entered when she didn't answer. The sight that greeted him brought him up short. Curled into a fetal ball, Elizabeth lay on the floor, tufts of Puffs scattered around her, and the box beside her. She was so still that Isaac thought she was asleep. Her back was to the door. He moved over to her, walking carefully on hardwood, grateful that it didn't creak as the floor in the house sometimes did.

He knelt on the floor and peered over her shoulder. She was staring straight ahead. It seemed like she was staring at the baseboard heat beneath the computer table but when he leaned further over her, he realized her eyes weren't focused. "Liz," he said gently.

She didn't answer. Her only response was the lowering of her eyelids. As he watched, a tear slid from the corner of her eye and hit the hardwood, making a teensy weensy puddle and creating a tiny splash zone.

"Come on, Babe," he said, gently raising her from the floor and cradling her against his chest. "The floor's too hard for you to lie on it, Liz. Let's get you to bed."

"I don't want to live, Isaac."

Isaac's heart missed countless beats. "Liz, don't say that. I love you and *I* want you to live," he encouraged her, his heart hammering now like crazy, fearful that she might become suicidal.

"I've tried to understand it but I can't, not really," she said brokenly, leaning on him hard.

Isaac plucked a tissue from the box and mopped her tears.

"I mean, how did this happen? What caused the placenta to break away?"

Isaac held her closer, unable to answer a question that Dr. Fields couldn't. "Liz, thinking about something with no answers is going to make the hurt worse. Don't think about it."

She pushed away from him suddenly. "How can I not think about it?" she demanded angrily, her voice turning shrill. "How can I not think about the child I lost?" She scrambled to her feet, and Isaac got up as well. "How can I not be confused, feel hurt, and want answers when my baby died and nobody knows why?" She glared at him, confusing Isaac with her sudden change. "How can I not feel the loss down here," she hit her ribs in the general region of her heart, "and way down here?" she hit her abdomen. "My child's lifeless body was sucked out of me." Her lips began to tremble at the memory, well the knowledge after the fact—she had no memory since she'd been under anesthesia—of the D & E, Dilation and Evacuation procedure she'd undergone to remove the baby. Isaac tried to take her in his arms to comfort her but she spun away from him as if she didn't want his touch. "How can I not feel great loss," she started again, wrapping her arms around her, her voice cracking with anguish, "when I know I'll never have another baby."

Isaac felt his body jerk as if a lightning bolt had hit it. The pain that tore through him left a burn, a piercing pain that seemed to grow with every breath for which he battled. Unsaid but understood between them was that Elizabeth wouldn't have another baby because of his inability to impregnate her, because of his inadequate manhood, because his sperm wasn't sufficient. He couldn't step up to the plate, couldn't meet the demand, couldn't do a man's job…just couldn't.

"Liz, I'm sorry," he said hoarsely. "I'm so sorry."

"It's not your fault," she whispered, sobbing. But when she ran from the room crying as if his presence reminded her of what she wanted but couldn't have, Isaac couldn't help but feel that it was his fault.

***

Meanwhile across town…

"Terence I—"

Her husband turned out the light while Sonja was speaking. She kept quiet for some beats, thinking it was accidental and he would turn it back on. He didn't. Annoyance filled up her chest, expanding to a huge and resentful lump of negativity towards this callous man to whom she was married. How come she hadn't seen this cold, unkind side of him while they were dating? Oh, she forgot, he was a great pretender, a master at hiding things—his true character and his cheating ways, only he wasn't quite slick, not perfect, with the last one. Almost five months ago, she'd intercepted a message he'd been sending in church and through Rose to Elizabeth Monroe, well Jones now. In it, he told the woman how much he missed her and wished she wouldn't marry that man. They could go back to old times. Pretty much, Sonja realized then that he'd had an affair with the woman. Of course, the note never got to Elizabeth. Sonja had kept it, not sure why. She'd thought about confronting him, but hadn't, fueling her anger instead into her exercise program. Then Rick had come along and started appreciating her, and she'd let it go. Deep in her heart, Sonja knew she'd entertained Rick's interest because of her anger towards her husband and his cheating.

Enough was enough. She'd let Terence's opinion control her life for far too long. Her exercise program had been motivated by a desire to lose weight for him, to get back the body he wanted. It should have been fueled by her desire to be healthy. She'd become interested in another man and nearly slept with him because her husband had neglected her emotional and sexual needs. She should have shut Rick down from his first attempt at flirtation because it was the right thing to do. She was married, and she respected God and herself. She should have attended to her spiritual needs and said no to Rick.

Tonight, in this moment, it would stop. She reached out and yanked the cord on the light switch of the lamp on her side of the bed. "In case you didn't notice, I was talking," she snapped.

"You don't need light to do that," he growled, pulling the covers over his head.

Sonja thought about yanking the comforter from him, but envisioned the childish tug of war that might ensue. She'd handle this in a dignified and adult way.

"Our wedding vows said for better or for worse. The Lord knows that I've been experiencing the worse for these past two years. About five months ago, I found out why."

He'd been puffing out put upon sighs until she said the last part.

"If you want to cheat, don't get our kids involved in it," she warned, measuring out her words as the memory of how he'd used Rose came back.

He threw off the comforter and tried to look confused. "What are you talking about?" he asked, sitting up.

Sonja's eyes skipped over him in disdain. He looked so ridiculous, trying to appear innocent when he was full of guilt. He ended up looking constipated. She got out of bed and took the note she'd kept all this time. By the time she finished reading, he had his head bowed. What could he say? She got him.

"That's what I'm talking about," she bit out. "Don't you EVER give our children notes to take to your girlfriends again."

"It's over," he admitted quietly.

Sonja snorted. "I should hope so. She's married, not that it mattered that *you* were when you were together. Anyway, I don't care either way. Starting right now, I'm going to do something that I should have done a long time ago. I'm going to care about me. I'm going to think of my needs, not yours. I'm claiming responsibility for my contentment rather than connecting my happiness to you."

His confusion was genuine this time.

"I'm talking about taking care of my health. I'm overweight, and I got this way because I haven't been eating right and exercising. I know I repel you, and you don't want to be with me because I'm heavy. At first, I started the weight loss to please you, but I'm at the point now where I'm doing it because it makes me feel good. That's the reason I should have done it in the first place and not for your approval. The only approval I need is from God. Whether I'm overweight, underweight, or the right weight, He loves me, which is what matters."

Sonja couldn't stop her tongue from saying the next even if it had been trussed up and tied down like a pig. "So you know, if you don't keep the home fires burning, somebody else will stoke them for you."

He head shot up like a popped bottle cap riding the fizz.

"Yes, and it's exactly what you think," she said at his widened eyes and shocked expression. Sonja watched his eyebrows flatten, then push down into a stormy frown. *Not so nice when the shoe is on the other foot and you're the one cheated on, is it?*

"Keep your cool," she said, laughing humorlessly. "I didn't go as far as you did. I would have, but the Holy Spirit wouldn't let me rest. I couldn't go all the way, so I let it go. But it won't happen again because I love God too much, respect myself a great deal, and believe in keeping my marriage vows—despite how painful that might be." She spared him a scathing glance. "So no, I didn't sleep with the guy, but I thought about it. One thing he made me realize, something that by your neglect and covert scorn I'd forgotten, is that I'm beautiful. My size isn't what makes me that way; my character, the way I treat a person and the way I talk to them is what makes me beautiful. I'll lose the weight, but not for you, never again for you, but for me. From this night going forward, we are husband and wife on paper only. I'm moving out of this room and into the guest room because I cannot be in the presence of negativity with the new me. I realize being under your disapproval has diminished my self-worth and respect, and broken me down emotionally. To heal, I want to limit my time around you."

Her husband stared at her as if she hadn't spoken English.

Sonja took her pillow and headed for the door.

"What about the children?" he called after her, sounding disoriented.

One hand on the door's handle, she turned to him and raised a careless eyebrow. "What about them?"

"What will they think when they realize we're not sleeping together?"

She shrugged. "Same thing they think when you don't hug me at worship, when you don't kiss me on Valentine's Day, or don't buy me flowers on my birthday—that you don't love me."

Sonja gave Terence a pitying smile as his mouth fell open. Some men were truly obtuse. Azalea already knew, or at least strongly suspected that he cheated. Rose and Dahlia noticed his distance with her. He was the only one living in a fool's paradise. She opened the door, stepped out, and closed it behind her. Surprisingly, her heart didn't feel a single prick of regret at the action she'd taken. She'd done the right thing. Sonja didn't know what the future held with Terence or if reconciliation were in the picture; she wouldn't close the doors to that. Her vows made before God were sacred to her. Either way it went, it was time to take care of herself, and that's what she was doing right now.

CHAPTER XX

Two months later at Connie's Café

"Didn't you hear me?" Elizabeth asked, swinging her gaze from Adrianna to Karen. "Isaac told me this morning that he wants a divorce."

"We heard you," Adrianna said, watching the contents of her teacup like something more than mint and honey was in it.

"We just don't understand why you're surprised," Karen said.

Elizabeth looked at her sister askance. "I don't know what motivated this."

Her sisters shared a look; Dri's gaze fell to the teacup again and Karen started studying the tablecloth with great interest.

"Okay, what is going on?" Elizabeth demanded, watching them with suspicion. "You know something that I don't. What is it?"

"Liz, your baby died, not your husband," Adrianna said frankly.

Elizabeth sat back in her chair, feeling hurt that her sister had brought up her pregnancy loss. "What's that supposed to mean?"

"Liz, how long are you going to grieve and ignore Isaac?" Karen put it plainly.

Elizabeth had suspected that Dri had been suggesting that she neglected her husband. Now that Karen confirmed it, she felt offended. "Did my husband complain to you?" she snipped.

"No, he complained to Douglas."

"Karen!" Adrianna exclaimed. "You weren't supposed to tell her that."

"She needs to know."

"Your husband is a minister," Elizabeth snapped. "Why is he sharing a parishioner's confidence with you?"

"Isaac spoke to him as a friend *and* brother-in-law, *not* as a pastor, so he spoke to me," Karen answered with spirit at her sister's condemning tone.

"So that you could talk to me," Elizabeth concluded, angry that her business had gone around the family information circuit before reaching her. Why hadn't her husband spoken to her if he felt neglected? "I don't understand why Isaac had to even go to Douglas. If he had a problem, he should have come to me."

"He didn't feel that you'd be receptive to him," Adrianna explained.

"Excuse me?" Elizabeth gave her a look full of attitude.

"Don't get upset with us," Adrianna said. "Since the baby died, you've been wrapped up in your own pain, so much so that you've said and done things to make your husband think him being with you will hurt you more than help you heal."

"Whaaat?!" Elizabeth exclaimed, confused now. "What are you talking about?"

"Why don't you make some time and go see your husband?" Karen suggested.

"And talk to him—the heart to heart kind," Dri added. "Find out what's on his mind and tell him what's on yours. Who knows, maybe with a little communication, you'll find yourself on the same page and divorce will turn into a hazy memory."

Elizabeth flashed a look between both girls and found their pointed expressions mirror images of one another. She glanced at her watch. It was ten-thirty. She drank the rest of the apple juice she'd ordered and wrapped up her bagel in a napkin.

She pushed her chair back and stood. "It seems that I'm the only one in the dark here. I don't suppose you're going to give me more details since you're shoving me to go talk to Isaac." She searched each sister's face. Both women shook their heads. "Okay. Since you're unwilling to shed light, I'll just go to the light source—my husband."

"Don't be mad at us for not giving details, Liz. It's something you need to find out from your husband," Karen said.

"Oh, I'm not mad," she denied. "Well, maybe a little annoyed that you know my husband's problem while I don't, but I know you care. I'll talk to you later." She kissed each sister on the cheek and hurried out of Connie's.

***

The Mountain Spring Atrium, a two-story business complex on Main Street in downtown Mountain Spring housed various professional offices—insurance, mortgage brokers, investment firms, architectural firms, and engineering firms to name a few. Structures and Designs Architecture, LLC was on the second floor of the Atrium. Elizabeth squeezed the Acura into a narrow space between a Ford truck and a Buick, hurried into the building, and took the elevator to the second floor.

She pulled open the glass door and entered the spacious office that housed the firm where her husband worked. The moment the red-haired Caucasian woman at the reception desk opened her mouth, Elizabeth realized it was the same woman who had coolly told her that Isaac was engaged, even though she'd identified herself as his wife and revealed the importance of the call on that day Terence had pulled the mischief.

"Hello, welcome to Structures and Designs. May I help you?"

I know where I am, Elizabeth thought sourly. *You don't have to identify the place. The name's in bold lettering on the glass doors, and I can read.* "I'm here to see Isaac Jones."

"I'm afraid Mr. Jones is engaged."

That again! How irritating!

"Do you have an appointment?"

"I don't need one. I'm his *wife.*"

"Oh," the woman said, looking taken aback while her green eyes flashed fire at Elizabeth's sharp response.

Say something, sister! Please say something! Liz had an earful to give her and was just waiting for the woman to spill some of the fire in her eyes. Elizabeth planned to throw some gasoline on it and blow the receptionist and this place up with the aggravation she was feeling.

She maintained her professionalism to Elizabeth's disappointment. "If you'll have a seat, I'll let him know that you are here." She gestured

113

to several grape and peach colored chairs in the reception area.

Elizabeth sat and waited about fifteen minutes before Isaac showed up in shirtsleeves and a black and gold print silk tie.

"Liz," he said inquiringly as he came towards her, "what are you doing here?"

"Missing you," she said softly and kissed him short and sweet, controlling herself because of their location. When she ended the kiss, he held her head in place and kept their lips in touch. It was only for a few moments, but his body language wasn't in sync with his request for divorce. His vibe didn't suggest that he wanted distance between them at all.

"Can we talk?" She asked the question low because she could see the nosy receptionist—Edna—straining to hear their conversation.

"Liz, I'm in the middle of a meeting? Can we do this tonight?"

She shook her head. That was too far away. "I can wait until you're done."

"It's that important?" he asked with a frown.

"*You're* that important," she said, smiling into his eyes, letting the love she held in her heart for him shine out.

He looked stunned for a moment, and then a slow smile eased his full lips into a smile that grew to devastating. "Come on, you can wait in my office," he invited.

***

A half hour later, they sat in adjacent chairs similar to the ones in reception, and before a wide mahogany desk that wasn't a traditional office desk. His computer was on it along with the usual office supplies, but Isaac said the majority of the surface was used to layout architectural plans, blueprints, and renderings.

"So why did you come to see me, Elizabeth?"

He hadn't called her that in a while. The many syllables in her name seemed to create the same amount of distance between them. "Liz," she corrected him.

"I'm sorry?"

"You called me Elizabeth. I want you to call me Liz. That doesn't create a gap between us."

Isaac looked at the floor, watching his linked hands dangle between his legs. "No, my infertility does that," he muttered.

"What did you say?" she asked, not hearing him clearly, or at least not sure that she had.

"What did you want to see me about?" he asked, side-stepping her question.

Elizabeth had been through many beginnings for this conversation she'd come to have with her husband. Up until this moment, she hadn't settled on one. She spoke the first words that came to her. "I'm sorry I ignored you these past two months."

The occasional swinging of his hands stilled. "I never said you did."

"You didn't have to. Deep down I was aware of it, but I wallowed in my own grief, dwelling on a past that's precisely that—an unchangeable history. My baby boy died, not my husband, not my man. I chose not to notice that with my neglect."

"He was my son, as well," he reminded her.

"I know, Isaac." She shifted her chair closer to her husband's and slid a hand across his shoulders. "I know how much you wanted him."

He laughed, a hollow empty sound. "You have no idea how much, Liz," he said quietly. "You told me once when we argued and before I accepted him that I should be thankful because I couldn't have one on my own. At the time, I was hurt by your duplicity and didn't see the truth of that. I woke up and did and developed a great hope to hold a child, gender unknown at the time, my child in my arms, knowing it would be my only one. Now, I'll never know what that feels like."

Elizabeth heard and felt the weight of regret in those words, his sorrow that he would never be a father. "I'm sorry, Isaac."

"That day when we lost him was terrible for me, but what was worse was the day I came home and found you curled up on the floor."

Elizabeth remembered that also.

"I'll never forget what you said before you ran from the room."

I'm sorry? Those were the words she remembered.

"You said you'll never have another baby," he told her. "Liz, when you said that, it hit me how critical to the continuance of our marriage my fertility had become. Before, there was hope for a child, but when it was taken away, I realized my inadequacy couldn't provide a replacement, even though you can't really replace a loss like that. At least, we could have another; but because of my inability, we can't." He covered his face and she heard him heave a huge breath, his shoulders rising and then falling on the exhalation. "Do you know how many times I've gone to the doctor since that night?"

He glanced at her, and then away. "Almost every week," he admitted. "I got my count checked regularly since that time, praying before I went to the doctor and hoping for a different outcome every time." He laughed bitterly. "You know what's funny in a pathetic sort of way? The sperm count kept falling instead of rising."

He said it was funny, but Elizabeth wasn't amused, and she could see that Isaac wasn't either.

"The doctor said I was under stress, trying to force something to happen that's supposed to occur naturally."

"They still don't know what's causing it, do they?" she asked. He'd said he didn't know the reason for his low sperm count when she'd asked him some time back.

He shook his head. "When I was small, I had mumps. That infection, the doctor says, may have caused an inflammation of the prostate that causes the low count."

"There are other ways to get pregnant," she suggested hesitantly.

"Like what?" The tenseness in his question was a clear indicator that he wasn't going to like her next statement.

Elizabeth said what she'd been thinking about, although she would only deign to use it as a last resort. "There are assistive reproductive techniques."

"No," he said flatly. "If I can't get you pregnant in the normal way, I'm not going to subject myself to that. It's clinical, cold, and not what God intended."

She didn't argue; Elizabeth thought the same thing. "We'll keep praying then," she encouraged.

"Liz, your desire for a baby isn't going to go away. My inability to give you one might never be reversed. God can perform a miracle, but He might choose not to. I've heard you these past few days praying and asking God for a child in the early hours of the morning."

When her eyes widened with surprise, he nodded. "I heard you. You thought I was sleeping, but I wasn't. Yet, while you prayed, you never accepted my advances, since our baby died, for us to be intimate. After a while, I started thinking that my infertility had killed your desire for intercourse with me, since you knew I couldn't impregnate you. Maybe you thought, what's the point?

"I'm at the place, Liz, where I'd rather be alone and loving you, rather than live under the same roof with you and not make love to you. I can't heal your hurt from the loss of our baby, Liz, and I may not be able to give you one, so I think it's best that we part ways."

He didn't look at her while he spoke, but watched the thickly woven burgundy carpet beneath his polished black shoes.

"Are you done telling me how you *think* I feel? Because if you are, then I can tell you how I *really* feel."

He turned his head and gave her a quizzical look. Elizabeth captured his gaze and began with a tiny smile, "I freely admit to being very selfish these past two months since the death of our baby, Isaac. I thought only about me and how I felt. As a result, I said things and acted in ways to push you away and created an emotional rift between us. I'm sorry for that, deeply and truly sorry." She leaned close and bussed his lips with hers.

"I remember saying that I'll never have another baby, and the truth is that it spilled from my lips because sorrow and regret for our loss was wracking my body. Did I at some level say that because I knew I might not get pregnant with you? More than likely, yes. Was it said to be spiteful towards you, to disdain you, or to hurt you? Definitely not. I love you, Isaac. I L-O-V-E you. I want only you, and if I had to do it all over again, I'd choose you, minus the duplicity and the courthouse marriage, of course. I'd also want a church wedding, if I did things over." She grinned and he smiled.

"Now, about not sleeping with you. That's a mistake that I intend to correct, starting tonight." She kissed him long, deep, and edgy when she saw desire jump in his eyes at her declaration. "I was out of it, couldn't even get the interest for the intimate side of life, because I was so mired in my grief. Several times after I lost the baby, I asked God why. One day last week the answer came to me very clearly and that's when I decided to put off 'sackcloth and ashes' and start living again. I remembered the story of David and Bathsheba. I remembered how David took her, another man's wife, and killed her husband, Uriah, breaking not one but two of God's commandments." Elizabeth smiled, a little sad but mostly accepting. "I remembered the child conceived in sin

117

and how it died. I thought back to how David lamented when the child was sick but ceased when the baby died."

"Liz," he started to protest, sensing her direction.

"Shush," she quieted him with a finger to his lips. "My situation is like David's with a gender role reversal. Like the song says, God has spoken, and now the church must say amen. God has spoken in my life, and I said amen."

Elizabeth took her husband's hand, rose from her chair, and tugged him out of his. She wrapped her arms around his neck and rested her forehead on his glad she was able to do that since they were equal in height with her three inch heels.

"Do you have any appointments in the next hour?"

He shook his head.

"No meeting?"

Negative again. Elizabeth's smile was broad. Things were working in her favor. "Can you take an early lunch?"

"Yes, where do you want to go?"

"Nowhere." She stepped out of his arms, leaving him bewildered, and went to close the blinds over the window, overlooking the outdoor garden in the center of the Atrium. "Lock the door," she instructed, "and tell the receptionist to hold your calls as you're lunching in."

He followed her orders to the letter. Elizabeth loved an obedient man. When she walked around the desk to stand before him once more, confusion had caved in to comprehension. Now he trained a predatory look full of passion on her. Isaac didn't wait for Elizabeth to step into his arms. He hauled her against his chest and wrapped his arms tightly around her.

"You promised to sleep with me starting tonight," he murmured huskily. "But I think, you intend to fast forward that plan."

"That would be correct," she whispered with a sultry smile, loosening his tie.

"So that you know, I didn't respond to your recent advances because my libido's been a little low from all your previous rejections of *my* advances," he said.

"I figured," Elizabeth murmured, touching her tongue to the corner of his mouth and dancing away when he came after her. She laughed at their play. "How's your libido right now?"

"Skyrocketing."

"Perfect, simply wonderful," she breathed, zeroing in on his mouth.

A breath before their kiss, he whispered, "I love you, Liz."

When their lips met she demonstrated the endearment that he'd spoken.

EPILOGUE

Two years later

"Uncle Isaac, Aunt Liz is sick," Nine-year-old Esther announced as he walked through the door with two large boxes of pizza.

Isaac frowned. "What's wrong with her?"

"She's throwing up."

He closed the door and set the pizza on the dining table. Casting a quick glance into the living room, he did a head count to ensure that all the kids were accounted for. Seven-year-old Jonah sat next to three-year-old Benjamin on the sofa, showing him some numbers game on the iPad. The little boy was fascinated and busily touching the screen and laughing when things happened. Jared and Aisha, both five years old, were watching Tarzan. It was Liz's favorite movie. He imagined she's the one who put that DVD in. He and Liz were watching Adrianna's and Karen's kids while they and their husbands went to a concert at the SAB church in Heart Haven. What a way to spend Saturday night? But he and Liz didn't mind. They enjoyed the children.

"Aunt Liz is in the bathroom?" he asked Esther.

The girl nodded. "May we have pizza?" she asked.

Esther was responsible. She could distribute. "Sure. Make sure everybody washes their hands in the guest bathroom, and use the disposable plates, okay?"

"Okay, Uncle Isaac," she agreed, hurrying to her siblings and cousins. "Pizza's here. Let's wash hands.

In the private bath off their bedroom, Isaac found Elizabeth seated on the edge of the tub with her head in her hands. There was a plastic bag beside her sock covered feet. Isaac hoped the regurgitated material wasn't in it. Her stomach had been upset yesterday as well. He prayed it wasn't a stomach virus, not with the kids here.

"Hey, Baby, what's wrong?"

She lifted her head at the sound of his voice and gave him a wan smile. "Nothing."

"Esther told me that you were throwing up."

"I'm fine now."

"Liz, you need to go to the doctor first thing on Monday. This might be serious."

"I'll do that." *It is serious—seriously good.* "Did you get the pizza?"

He nodded. "Esther is sharing for everyone."

"She's such a blessing."

Isaac flipped the toilet's lid down and sat. "I guess no pizza for you then."

She grimaced and shook her head. "As a matter of fact, I'll stay in here until you're done eating."

"I hope it's not something contagious," Isaac worried. "We don't want them to go home sick when they came here well."

"Oh, they'll be all right."

"How can you be sure?" he pressed, still concerned.

"Because of these." She handed the plastic bag at her feet to him.

Isaac took it gingerly, figuring it wasn't vomit if she was offering it so eagerly, but still being careful. He peeked inside and his eyes popped. Scrabbling like a mad man, he pulled out the two test sticks, and stared at the two bright pink lines on each stick. He gained his feet on rubbery legs.

"Is this…" he stopped and swallowed, cautious hope feeling like ballooning joy in his chest at his wife's wide smile.

"Yes! We're pregnant!" she exclaimed, not waiting for him to finish his question.

Isaac dropped the strips, pulled his wife to him, swung her up into his arms, and spun around crazily in the bathroom.

"That's why you're throwing up," he asked, sounding dazed as he set her back on her feet.

Elizabeth nodded, giggling with happiness.

Isaac covered his face and started breathing hard into his hand.

"Are you okay, sweetheart?" Elizabeth asked, hoping he wasn't hyperventilating.

"I just need a minute," he said, his answer muffled.

He took several more deep breaths, and she heard a few sniffles. Elizabeth's eyes started to burn at the realization that her husband was crying. She understood how emotional this was for him; it had been for her when she discovered it earlier. For both of them, it was an answer to prayer; for him, it was a true miracle because his sperm count had not increased in the past two years. This was a direct answer from God.

His eyes were red and wet when he uncovered his face. Elizabeth handed him the tissue she'd pulled from the roll. He wiped his eyes, blew his nose, and washed his hands. Composed now, his voice nevertheless, came out a bit raspy when he asked, "How do you feel?"

"Beyond the upset stomach, I'm fine," Elizabeth told him, smiling and stepping into his open arms.

"God is..." Isaac stopped and shook his head, searching for a word.

"Indescribable," Elizabeth supplied.

"Behold I am the Lord, the God of all flesh; is anything too difficult for me?" Isaac repeated God's words in Jeremiah 32:27. "No, Lord, nothing," he answered the rhetorical question and whispered a prayer of thanksgiving in the same breath. "Lord, thank You for your love and mercy towards us. Thank You for answered prayers, and Lord, thank You for the grace and kindness You've shown to me." Together, he and Elizabeth murmured 'amen' at the same time Esther called, "Are you guys coming for pizza?"

"Can you manage to go out there?" he asked, understanding that the cheesy smell might bother her.

"I'll try. The kids are going to be excited to hear this news."

The screaming and jumping following the announcement took excitement to a new level. Esther called her mother and handed the phone to Elizabeth. Her sisters nearly broke her eardrums with the screeching. Douglas and Christopher called Isaac. Elizabeth had no idea what they said to him, but from his laughter, she knew it was all good things.

Nine months later, on the eve of the Sabbath, Jacob and Crystal Jones were born to an exhausted but contented mother and to a father who had possibly maxed out his iPhone memory from all the pictures he took and saved of his newborn babies. As Isaac looked at his children, he thought that God had closed a door and opened up windows of blessings for him. He served an awesome God.

EXCERPTS FROM OTHER SENECA MOUNTAIN SERIES TITLES

A Fall for Grace
(Seneca Mountain Romances: Book 1)
<u>Excerpt</u>

"Solomon, this isn't going to work. I can't—."

"Shh," he said, silencing her negatives and pessimism with a finger against her lips. "I love you," he declared and then repeated it, enunciating the words so there would be no incomprehension, "*I love you*. And I'm not going to let you throw what we have and all we can have away. The Bible tells us to ask, seek, and knock and doors will open for us. I am going to keep asking, seeking, and knocking until you open your heart to me. I'm going to be like that widow who the judge got tired of and just gave her what she wanted. You're the judge. Consider me the petitioner. I'm not going to stop telling you that I love you, that I need you, that I refuse to live my life any more without you until you get tired, surrender and give me what we both want and need."

Looking into his eyes, Grace was captivated by the determination in those dark depths. The intensity of his speech and the sincerity of his words were breaking through the invisible walls of resistance that she'd erected. If he kept at it tonight, she wasn't sure she'd last with this battle against the onslaught of his love. Could she really take a chance on him? Should she take a chance on him? Would she have regrets later if she let him go? If she yielded to the pull and poignancy of this moment, and accepted the love he'd declared, received the permanence with him that he was offering, would she have regrets later?

He pulled her into his arms, letting her feel the hardness of him against her tender places, stirring desire in her heart and in places that should stay asleep until wedded bliss. He kissed the corner of her mouth. "Take a chance on me Grace," he coaxed, his voice a seductively husky sound. It was like he'd read her mind. She felt the foundations of her fortress give way and begin crumbling. "You won't regret it," he promised and whatever barriers she'd set up against him buckled under the weight of his persistence. "I love you, Grace." In her heart, she whispered the same. Aloud she promised to take a chance on him for the second time that week.

A Price Too High
(Seneca Mountain Romances: Book 2)
<u>Excerpt</u>

As it turned out, he was speechless when he opened the door and saw her, but then so was she. The sight of him in a ridged undershirt that outlined every muscle on his chest and showcased his powerful biceps tumbled her thoughts into a steamy memory of tangled sheets, urgent kisses, frenzied caresses, and the mind-blowing passion that they had shared on their sole night together.

He was staring at her stomach like it was a UFO and this was his very first time seeing one. If their roles were reversed, maybe she would be shocked too. Karen passed her tongue over her lips and forced herself to speak. "Hi, Douglas. May I come in?"

Shock sped away fast. His eyes jumped from her belly to her face and the fury blazing in his gaze made Karen cringe. "You lying, scheming, wicked user!" Every vitriolic word barreled through his clenched teeth and slammed Karen like assault weapons' firepower, each hit leaving her fighting for breath and struggling to stay on her feet with the unmasked hatred in them. His voice rising, he accused, "You *left* me on our wedding night, skulking away like a thief without having the decency or courage to tell me to my face how you truly felt about my family and why you had really married me. You sent me an inadequate text message after you fled, leaving me reeling and wondering how you could say you love me, how you could make love with me and then use me as a vessel for revenge. You never returned my numerous calls and then you disconnected your phone. Now seven months later you show up at my door and expect *me* to let *you* in?"

Tears, hot and stinging pooled in her eyes, and her throat ached with the effort not to cry out at the scorn and disdain in her husband's face. She hadn't expected a positive reception, but neither had she been prepared for the magnitude of his venom. By force of will alone, she managed to keep her tears at bay, but her voice still wobbled when she spoke. "I-I n-need to talk to you, Doug. P-please let me in."

He looked at her for a long time, the repugnance in his expression unchanged, before he turned and walked back into the apartment, leaving the door open. Karen bit her lip, thinking that the open door meant she could enter. She crossed the threshold with cautious steps.

All Things Work Together
(Seneca Mountain Romances: Book 3)
<u>Excerpt</u>

I want to talk to you about Adam."

Jasmine's spine stiffened. She knew where this wind was blowing. "What about him?" she asked calmly.

He sat back in his office chair and folded his arms across his chest. "He told me that you confiscated his phone last night."

"Did he tell you why?" Jasmine raised her eyebrows, the question flavored a bit with spunk.

"He was on it after curfew, but th—"

"For the third night in a row," she interrupted, emphasizing the magnitude of the misdeed.

"Yes, I know all that, but that's not the part I have a problem with."

"Oh?" There were parts to this now? And why would he have a problem? Hadn't he been concerned about her maintaining order in his household? Now he had a problem when she fulfilled his wishes?

"When Adam got his phone back there were three international calls made from it. Two to Jamaica and one to St. Thomas."

Jasmine sat statue-still in her chair, hearing the accusation he hadn't articulated. She raised a forefinger, "Wait one minute. If there were international calls on his phone, I didn't make them."

"The times of the calls were when you had the phone in your possession," he pointed out.

He still hadn't accused her outright, but he didn't have to. He believed she made those calls. That was clearer than day. Adam King, Jr. was a crafty boy. She hadn't expected this. Jasmine wouldn't underestimate him again, but if he thought he could intimidate her into not enforcing the rules his dad put in place, he'd better think twice. But first things first. One problem at a time. "Look, Pastor King, I just told you I did not make those calls. Obviously, you don't believe me. The fact that you've persisted with the issue by pointing out that I had the phone at the times of the calls, implying that no other person could have made the calls, tells me that you'll believe your son's word over mine. I understand that. I'm a stranger still, and he's your child. However, you might want to consider a couple of things: I have my own phone. Why would I use your son's? The day we met, you doubted whether I understood teenagers or whether I could care for them. At the risk of being insubordinate, I'm now wondering how much *you* understand teenagers?"

He leaned forward in his chair, his expression hard. The chill in his eyes said her words had struck a chord. Jasmine wasn't trying to get fired, but she'd learned it's best to start as you mean to go on. Don't take things docilely, especially when you're not at fault. Be firm, frank, and as much as possible be polite, but speak your mind.

"Have you considered that Adam was the one who made those calls?" she asked.

"Why would he do that?" His tone could turn a water droplet to an icicle.

"Because he was angry that I took his phone, he wanted to get back at me. He probably hoped to intimidate me into not doing it again if he got me in trouble with you."

"You don't know my children like I do, Ms. Lewis. Adam isn't the kind of child to be cunning like that," he objected.

"Sometimes I wonder if you know your children at all, Pastor." Okay she was having a problem with the 'be polite' part. Now the words were out, and she could not take them back. Jasmine didn't try to fix it because she couldn't.

"What's that supposed to mean?" His eyebrows went south and his mouth firmed into a displeased line, annoyance shadowing his expression like storm clouds darkening the skies.

"You work all the time. They don't see you. Do you know that Claire wishes you worked fewer hours so you could spend more time with her? Do you know that Adam sleeps restlessly some nights and cries out for you?" She watched surprise and hurt do a fast exchange in his expression before he camouflaged it. "And do you know that he also cries out for his mother?"

"Enough!" The word struck like thunder, cracking the air like lightning.

Jasmine jerked and watched pain and anger perform a visible struggle in his face. He inhaled a significant portion of the oxygen in the air and exhaled slowly. "I might not know everything there is to know about my kids," he started, his voice tight and his words measured. "And maybe I do need to spend time with them," he continued through his teeth. "But you don't know them period. You don't know any of us. You have no idea what we've been through as a family, what we still go through. Do me a favor and clear it with me before you punish my kids and please don't ever mention their mother again. Goodnight, Ms. Lewis." With that, he left his chair and opened the door.

Stunned, she sat there for some moments before grasping that this was a dismissal. She rose slowly and approached the door with even more lethargic steps. At the door she paused, not sure what to say, but feeling compelled to make an exit statement. She looked up at him, but he was staring determinedly at some point beyond her, his jaw like granite. Jasmine wet her lips. "I'm sorry. I didn't mean to stir up old hurts. I was just trying to—"

"Good. Night. Ms. Lewis." The words came out with forceful pace, the emotion in them bordering on violence.

Jasmine sailed out the door. She knew when she had overstayed her welcome.

A Matter of Trust
(Seneca Mountain Romances: Book 4)
<u>Excerpt</u>

Adrianna threw up her hands. "Are you listening to yourself? You're talking about the woman as if she's still alive. You're not going to let me 'paint her' with my wrongdoing? I can't paint her with anything. She's dead, DEAD. And if you want this marriage to last, you'll recognize that she is D-E-A-D!"

"If *I* want this marriage to last," he asked, his tone low, deadly, and dangerous.

Adrianna swallowed and scrambled mentally to regroup. In her anger, she'd said the wrong thing. But she was tired of Cindy's shadow and couldn't take it anymore.

"You'd better consider if you even have a marriage. You have single handedly destroyed my trust in you by what you did. I don't trust you, Adrianna, and if I don't trust you, what sort of relationship will we have? Not much of one. And if we don't have a relationship, my question to you is this: Do we have a marriage?"

Dri clutched her throat and tried to hide the tremor shaking her frame. Was he thinking of divorce?

ABOUT THE AUTHOR

A believer in happy endings and forever after type stories, Brigette has been an avid romance reader since her teens. Inspired by her own real life romance with her husband, Clifford, she began writing romance novels after the birth of her first child and hasn't stopped since. Brigette holds a degree in Cultural Studies with a concentration in communication. Brigette writes Christian Romance and Christian Romantic Suspense. She lives in the northeastern U.S.A. with her husband and four children. She can be reached at her website, http://www.brigettemanie.com/contact-us-newsletter-sign-up/ to sign up for her newsletter and giveaways. You can also find her at the links below:

https://www.facebook.com/brigette.manie.author?ref=stream
https://twitter.com/BrigetteManie

CPSIA information can be obtained at www.ICGtesting.com
Printed in the USA
LVOW06s2138260715

447744LV00008B/118/P